THE
CHIP SHOP
GHOST

Tim, Dorothy and Stephen have a problem. A ghost has appeared from nowhere – he knits, he wears electric purple suits and when alive he was a magician!

The Great Porrex is back to find his magician's wand, and doesn't seem to mind how long it takes to find it . . . In desperation the children strike a bargain. If they find the wand, the ghost must agree to teach the bullies who terrorise their street a lesson. But is the Great Porrex just a ghostly con-man? Will he be able to keep his side of the bargain? The children will just have to wait and see . . .

With this very funny story, Eileen Dunlop has written her first book for younger children, although she is well-known and respected for older fiction.

Born in Alloa, she has always lived in Scotland, and many of her books have Scottish themes or backgrounds.

THE CHIP SHOP GHOST

Eileen Dunlop

Illustrated by Ben Cort

Blackie

For John Whitehead

Copyright © 1991 Eileen Dunlop
Illustrations © 1991 Ben Cort
First published 1991 by Blackie and Son Ltd

A CIP catalogue record for this book is available from
the British Library.

ISBN 0 216 93067 7

Blackie and Son Ltd
7 Leicester Place
London WC2H 7BP

Printed in Great Britain

Contents

1   An Unusual Tea-Time

The Ghost arrived by bus. When the concertina doors wheezed open outside the Portly Puss pet shop on the corner of Baltic Street, he alighted gracefully, wafted along the pavement like a little breeze among the shoppers, and entered at the open door of the Tartan Parrot café. It was half-past four, on a pleasant September afternoon.

Mrs Bonella was standing at the fish-fryer in her flowery apron, rhythmically dipping fillets of cod in batter, to be ready for the early evening rush-hour. She saw nothing, but she was aware of a cold draught blowing past her, stirring the fringed plastic curtain which separated the shop from the little restaurant behind. So she went and closed the door, then got on with her work.

Just after five o'clock, Tim and Dorothy saw the Ghost. They had been in the flat upstairs, doing their homework, until the scent of the first batch of fresh fish and chips floated up to them, reminding their noses that it was time for tea.

'I'll have hamburger and chips, Mum,' said Dorothy, clattering into the shop through the door

marked 'Private'.

'Fish for me,' said Tim. 'And chips, and a pickled onion, and tomato ketchup, and a Coke, and—'

'Where's your manners?' asked Mrs Bonella automatically, as she shovelled food onto cardboard plates. She didn't approve of eating off cardboard, but it saved washing up, and nobody else in Baltic Street seemed to mind. 'What's the magic word?'

'Please,' they said, also automatically.

Then they escaped with their trays through the coloured plastic fronds of the curtain, and were surprised, so early in the evening, to find that they did not have the restaurant to themselves.

He was sitting at one of the little formica-topped tables, under the mural of the Bay of Naples which Grandpa Bonella had once had painted, to remind him of the scenes of his childhood. At first glance, the stranger did not look very ghost-like, although his face was very thin and pale. With his black beard and whiskers, purple velvet suit and electric-blue silk tie, he was unusual for Baltic Street, that was all. On the chair beside him he had a bag made of carpet material, with a leather handle.

Dorothy and Tim sat down at a table opposite, and began to eat, watching him with their dark, Italian eyes. Tim had dark hair, too, but Dorothy had thick fair curls, of which she was very proud.

'Maybe he's on his way to a party,' suggested Dorothy in a whisper.

'Go on! He's just a big jessie,' replied Tim, not bothering to whisper. 'Just look at all those flashy rings!' Dorothy was embarrassed.

'Shut up, Tim,' she muttered. 'He'll hear you!'

But if he did, he paid no attention. He fidgeted and sighed, looking around him with pale eyes, and flicking invisible specks of dust off his sleeve with long, ringed, white fingers. He picked up the greasy menu-card, glanced at it, and put it down again.

'Excuse me,' said Dorothy after a few minutes of this. 'I don't suppose you realise. There's no

service in the restaurant until Gilly comes on duty at half-past six. If you want something to eat, you'll have to fetch it on a tray from the counter.'

Slowly, the strange figure swivelled round, and two bleached-blue eyes glared at the children. But it was not the intensity of their look that made Tim and Dorothy freeze, forks suspended half-way between their cardboard plates and their open mouths. All of a sudden, they were noticing something else. Through his chest they could see little yachts sailing on the Bay of Naples, and through his head the distant Island of Capri.

'It's a ghost,' squeaked Tim. Dorothy was speechless. She looked at the transparent man with an interest so complete that she even forgot that ghosts are supposed to make you afraid. Then the Ghost spoke.

'Of course I'm a ghost,' he said, in a cross but ordinary voice, without spooky quavers. 'How can I be anything else? I've been dead for ninety years. And I don't want anything to eat. What I want is my magic wand. I lost it on the night when I was – er, called away unexpectedly, and I want it back. See?'

Of course, they did not see. Tim and Dorothy gaped at him, trying to think of something appropriate to say, but before they could, the Ghost continued peevishly, 'It's so provoking! All these years I've thought I had only to come back, shimmer down beneath the stage, and pick it up.

11

I was convinced it would have been overlooked in the drama of my Last Great Exit. There must have been other things to think about in that scene of horror, goodness knows.'

Tim picked out the only word in all this that he understood. 'Listen, Mr – um, Ghost,' he said. 'I think you must have come to the wrong place. There's no stage here. This is a café, you see.' He rather hoped that the Ghost would realise his mistake, and vanish. Then Tim could get on with his tea, which was getting cold.

The Ghost gave him a chilling look. 'I have not come to the wrong place,' he retorted. 'I may be dead, but I'm not stupid. When I made my Last Great Exit on that fatal night in 1900, on this spot stood the Baltic Theatre, the finest Palace of Varieties north of the Border. Such nights of song and laughter! Such pantomimes! Such entertainment! You would have thought the place was built to stand for ever. But when I come back, a mere ninety years later, what do I find?' He clasped his forehead in a dramatic fashion. 'Gone, all gone! And in its place, a tawdry eating-house! Fried potatoes! Stinking fish! No oysters, no eel pie!'

'He's away with the birds,' said Dorothy sadly.

'He's a rude old bogey-man!' exclaimed Tim indignantly. Hearing the reputation of the Tartan Parrot attacked, he quite forgot that you were supposed to be terrified of ghosts. 'Stinking fish! I'll give him stinking fish down his trousers if he

12

doesn't watch out!'

Dorothy quailed. She was about to apologise hastily for Tim, but then she realised that the Ghost showed no sign of rising up in wrath and striking her brother down. Instead, with a hopeless gesture, he bowed his head, and there was a sob in his voice as he replied, 'Forgive me. I did not mean to offend. This is all so very upsetting, you know. I was so looking forward to a good haunting, a chin-wag by moonlight with a theatrical fellow-ghost or two, and above all, to recovering my wand. It's all so disa-pp-pp-pointing!' The children heard another sob. Then the Ghost took out a diaphanous handkerchief, and blew his diaphanous nose.

Tim and Dorothy looked at each other, and took a fateful decision. After all, they thought, a ghost who snivelled in his hanky could not be very dangerous.

'Look,' said Dorothy kindly. 'You'd better come upstairs with us, and we'll see if there's anything we can do to help. The café will be getting busy soon, and Mum doesn't like people sitting at tables if they're not eating.'

'Just what I was thinking,' agreed Tim. 'Come on – we'll take you up the back stairs.'

2 The Great Porrex

Once he was settled in an armchair by the electric fire in the Bonellas' living-room, with his carpet-bag at his side, the Ghost put away his hanky, and cheered up a bit. He unrolled his long, insubstantial legs across the hearth-rug, looked curiously at the television set, and made a few polite remarks about the tapestry picture of Edinburgh Castle, which Mrs Bonella had made the winter she broke her leg, and had a nice long holiday from the café.

Tim and Dorothy sat on the couch opposite, noticing that now they could see the pattern on the rug through his feet, and the ornaments on the sideboard through his head. Tim thought that he was like a coloured glass bottle, shaped like a person. So far, there was nothing very scary about him, and, knowing that their mother would be busy downstairs for many hours to come, the children relaxed. It was funny how quickly you could become accustomed to having a real dead ghost in your living-room.

'Names?' enquired the Ghost presently.

'Dorothy,' said Dorothy.

'Tim,' said Tim.

'Porrex,' said the Ghost. He paused expectantly, then added significantly, 'The Great Porrex.' They sensed that he was waiting for them to respond.

'How do you do?' said Dorothy.

The Ghost raised his eyebrows. He looked surprised and mortified at the same time. 'Do you mean to tell me,' he asked incredulously, 'that my name means nothing to you? Have you really never heard of The Great Porrex?'

The children had to confess that they had never heard of any Porrexes, great or small. The Ghost took this badly.

'Is it possible,' he enquired sniffily, 'that I have been forgotten, after only ninety years? Is it possible that even small fry like you have never heard of Porrex, who topped the bill in every theatre in the land?' Receiving no answer, he went on, 'And what about all the other great performers who took the stage with me? Vesta Tilley, Chung Ling Soo, Harry Lauder, Marie Lloyd? I suppose you've never heard of them either?'

'I've heard of Harry Lauder,' said Tim, hoping to please. 'He was a Scots comedian – a funny wee man in a kilt, with a daft bonnet and a walking-stick. He was famous.'

It was the wrong thing to say. The Ghost did not want to hear that anyone else's fame had outlasted his.

'He was a passable performer,' he replied stiffly, 'although of course my talents were vastly superior.'

'Sorry,' said Tim, trying not to laugh. He was finding the Ghost more comical with every passing minute. But the Ghost looked as if he were going to cry again, and once more Dorothy felt sorry for him. So she asked him the question which she was sure he was longing to be asked.

'What exactly were your talents, Mr Porrex? Do tell us. We'd love to know.'

The Ghost gave Dorothy a grateful look, and leaned forward in his chair. 'Young lady,' he said,

'I was a magician, a conjuror, an illusionist. The greatest.' And smiling reminiscently, he began to boast about his career in the variety theatres of Queen Victoria's time.

Other magicians had sawn people in half, but Porrex had sawn them in quarters. Other magicians had conjured white doves out of the air, but Porrex's doves had been red, white and blue. He had performed the Indian rope trick with a lighted candle on his head, he had hypnotised a duchess, and made her dance the Highland Fling. He had floated in the air in the presence of the Prince of Wales, and he had made a ghost appear, causing terror in the audience at London's Tivoli Music Hall. He had had imitators, but no equals. He was The Greatest.

Dorothy and Tim had never heard such bragging in their lives. Dorothy was mildly shocked, while Tim was more amused than ever.

'Was it a real ghost, the one at the Tivoli Music Hall?' he wanted to know, when at last he could get a word in edgeways. He was tickled at the notion of a ghost conjuring up another ghost, but then he remembered that at the time, this ghost hadn't been a ghost.

'An illusion,' the Ghost assured him airily. 'All done with mirrors. Easy if you know how.'

As if one ghost in an evening were not enough, Tim would have liked to ask for a demonstration. But before he could annoy the Ghost by asking for one, Dorothy cut in with another question.

'Mr Porrex,' she said, 'I was wondering. How did you come to lose your magic wand?'

'Ah, yes, my wand.' Recalled from memories of his past triumphs, the Ghost lay back in his chair, put the tips of his spectral fingers together, and heaved a sigh. 'Alas,' he said. 'It was a fine wand, which had once belonged to my great-uncle Ferrex, also a grand magician in his day. It would have been careless to lose it, in any other circumstances.' The children waited expectantly, and after more dramatic sighing, the Ghost went on.

'It was the night of 27th December, in the year 1900. I was top of the bill, naturally, in a seasonal entertainment at the Baltic Theatre, which stood then where your family eating-house stands now. As the climax to my act, I was to disappear from a cabinet which I had entered loaded with chains. So as to have my hands free, I slipped the wand into the pocket of my coat, this very coat I am wearing now. I have the pocket, but I never saw the wand again.'

'Why not?' demanded Dorothy.

'I shall explain,' promised the Ghost. 'But first I must tell you that on that night, I gave my last performance, and the curtain came down on my distinguished career. Under the cabinet, there was a trap-door in the stage, through which I was supposed to vanish after removing my chains. This would have been the work of seconds, had it

not been for the incompetence of my assistant, Miss Pussy Katz—'

'Miss Pussy Katz,' gurgled Tim, but fortunately the Ghost did not notice the interruption.

'It was Pussy's task,' he went on seriously, 'to bind me with chains, but to close the padlock very lightly, so that I could open it with a flick of my finger. After shutting me in, she was to talk to the audience and divert their attention, until I signalled that I was free. Then she had to press the button which opened the trap-door, so that I could climb down the ladder, run round the back of the stage, and come on again to rapturous applause. Instead the silly girl closed the padlock so tightly that I could not undo the chains, then, thinking that she had missed my signal, she pressed the button. Unable to use the ladder, I fell thirty feet to instantaneous death. A dramatic exit,' the Ghost concluded, with a tiny smirk of satisfaction, 'although a premature one.'

'How terrible,' said Dorothy. 'I expect the wand dropped out of your pocket when you fell.' The Ghost nodded.

'Yes,' he said. 'When I recovered from the shock of being – translated I believe is the correct word, I found that I still had my pocket-book, my tooth-pick, my snuff-box and my cigars. But the wand was lost in the darkness beneath the stage.'

'What happened to Pussy Katz?' asked Tim eagerly. 'Was she tried for your murder?'

'No,' replied the Ghost bitterly, 'although she should have been. It was "death by misadventure", they said, and Pussy got off scot-free. Not long ago she celebrated her one hundred and eighth birthday in a Rest Home in Liverpool. There's no justice in the world.'

Neither of the children could think how to answer this, but in any case, just then there was a diversion. While they talked, it had begun to get dark, and now, in the street outside, there was a sudden glare of hard, moving light. A wild roaring of powerful engines ripped through the air, as a pack of motor-cycles sped past the Tartan Parrot, screeched round the roundabout at Dockland

Cross, and shot back on the other side of the road. Dorothy jumped up, and ran to the window.

'Oh, dear,' she cried in dismay, peering out between the net curtains. 'It's those dreadful Phantoms again. I hope it isn't our turn for a visit.'

'Phantoms?' repeated the Ghost, puzzled. 'What Phantoms?'

'Not your kind,' Tim assured him. 'They're bikers – Hell's Angels – you know.' The Ghost did not know.

'There are no angels in hell,' he said flatly. 'You can take it from me.'

'They're a gang,' Tim explained. 'There are six of them, and they call themselves the Phantoms. They go about frightening people.'

'Are they dead?' asked the Ghost, now thoroughly confused.

'No, they're alive,' said Tim. 'They just call themselves Phantoms. They have skulls and crossbones painted on their leather jackets. Sometimes they come into the shop, and threaten to break it up if Mum doesn't give them fish and chips without paying.'

'Are they hungry?' asked the Ghost.

'Not a bit,' Dorothy told him, her round cheeks pink with annoyance. 'Two of them live down in Harbour Lane, which isn't much of a place, but they're not poor people. And the rest live in posh houses up in Oslo Avenue. Pinky Mackintosh's father is a dentist, and Jake Gorman was at the

Queen's Academy before they threw him out for coming to school drunk, and threatening the teachers. They're not hungry, Mr Porrex, they're just bad.'

'But this is scandalous,' said the Ghost indignantly. 'That sort of thing gives decent, self-respecting phantoms a bad name. Has your mother summoned the Constabulary?'

'Who? Oh, you mean the police,' said Tim. 'No. Too scared. Everybody's scared of the Phantoms around here.' The Ghost said no more, but he looked thoughtful.

'They're parked on the other side of the street,' announced Dorothy from the window. 'They're going into the Golden Dragon. Poor Mrs Cheng!'

'At least it isn't poor Mrs Bonella's turn tonight,' said Tim glumly. All the fun had been knocked out of him.

But suddenly, the Ghost seemed to have lost interest. 'Time for me to go, I think,' he said, picking up his carpet-bag, and rising smoothly to his feet. 'Since there is no theatre, I must look for other accommodation nearby. A church, perhaps, or a nice ruin. But we shall meet again soon.'

'Shall we?' asked Dorothy, turning away from the window.

'Oh, yes,' the Ghost assured her. 'Have no doubt. I have not forgotten your kind offer of help in the search for my wand.'

Then he disappeared through the wall.

3 The Ghost's Bargain

Next morning, when they were having breakfast at a table in the corner of the restaurant, Tim said through a mouthful of cornflakes, 'Mum, before the Tartan Parrot was built, do you remember what building stood here?'

The previous evening's meeting with the Ghost now seemed so preposterous that, if Dorothy had not shared it, he would have dismissed it as a peculiar dream. Even so, he wondered whether a shared dream were not the more believable explanation. If his mother had said, 'A church,' or, 'A hotel,' he would have thought that yesterday's school sausages had given them stomach upsets.

Mrs Bonella looked at him across the table with dark, tired eyes. She used to be a happy, cheerful woman, but recently life in Baltic Street, with its vandals, and untrained dogs, and litter, and noise, and now the Phantoms, had been getting her down. She slept badly, and had no patience, even with her children, whom she loved.

'Eight o'clock in the morning,' she said wearily, 'and you want a history lesson. What does it matter what was here before the café? Why d'you want to know?'

'A project,' lied Tim. You could always get information out of Mrs Bonella if you said it was for a project. She believed in education, which could get you out of Baltic Street. It was idle questions that irritated her. 'A project,' said Tim, 'about the street where I live.' It worked, as usual.

'Well, if it's important. It was a theatre,' Mrs Bonella told him. 'It was still standing when I was a little girl, although it was derelict – a terrible eyesore of a place, all boarded-up and covered with graffiti and torn old posters. What was it called, now? The Baltic, I think. It must have been demolished about 1964, and the shops built just after that, because Grandpa moved into this one in 1966.'

'So you were never actually inside the theatre, Mum?' asked Tim.

She looked at him, half amused and half annoyed. 'Do me a favour, Tim. The place was closed down before the Second World War, and I wasn't born till 1955. Who d'you think I am? Queen Victoria?'

'Do you think he'll come back?' asked Dorothy, when Mrs Bonella had gone out to the kitchen to fetch some more milk.

Tim shrugged his shoulders. 'If you'd asked me when we got up, I'd have said no, because we'd dreamed the whole thing,' he replied. 'But what

Mum just told us fits in so well with what he told us, now I'm not so sure. We'll just have to wait and see.'

They did not have to wait for very long.

When they got home from school that afternoon, the shop was not yet open. Tim and Dorothy let themselves in by the house-door, took off their coats, and went upstairs to the flat. When they opened the living-room door, the most extraordinary sight met their eyes.

Mrs Bonella was sitting on the couch with her shoes off, and her feet up, watching her favourite television programme. Nothing unusual about

that. What was unusual, was that less than a metre away from her, in the best armchair, reclined the Ghost, looking very much at home with one leg crossed over the other. He was knitting a luminous green scarf, on two long knitting-needles, drawing up lengths of wool from a ball at the bottom of his carpet-bag. He paused, wiggled his fingers at the children, and made a 'Sh-sh' shape with his lips. Not that Tim and Dorothy needed the warning. They were too thunder-struck to say a word.

'Hello,' said Mrs Bonella, fortunately too engrossed in the programme to take her eyes off the screen. If she had, she would have seen Tim and Dorothy looking as if they had seen a ghost. 'Had a good day?'

The children managed to say that it had been okay. Deciding that they had better act as normally as possible, they sat down and pretended to watch too. Tim grimaced sideways, jerking his thumb towards the door, but the Ghost ignored the hint. He plied his needles busily, pulling out his wool and counting stitches under his breath. At one point he took out a measuring-tape, and measured his scarf in inches.

Her programme finished, Mrs Bonella sighed, took her feet off the couch, and groped with her toes for her slippers. She got up, and switched off the television.

'Do your homework. Feed the cats,' she said,

and left the room, her wide skirts brushing against the Ghost's chair as she passed. The children were left staring at the Ghost, who said, 'Two plain, two purl, two plain,' and yanked up another length of hideous wool.

'She didn't see you,' Dorothy gasped.

The Ghost shrugged. 'Obviously not,' he replied. 'Grown-up people never do – that is, unless I choose to reveal myself. Children always see me. Some not-very-bright ones, like yourselves, take some time to see through me—' Tim sniggered, and received one of the Ghost's chilling looks '—and many are too dense ever to do so at all. But the most sensitive realise what I am straight away.'

The truth of this was just about to be demonstrated. As the Ghost finished speaking, they heard through the half open living-room door, the sound of the house door downstairs being opened. A voice called, 'Tim! Are you in?'

Mrs Bonella's voice said, 'Oh, it's you, Stephen. Go on up, then. Tim's in the living-room.'

There were light, running steps on the stairs, and before Tim had time to think of stepping in front of the Ghost, Stephen Cheng, his chum from across the street, stood in the doorway. He was holding a football to his chest.

'Tim, do you want to play—' he began brightly. But then his voice faltered, and his long black eyes widened as he gazed past his friend at the

apparition sitting in the armchair. 'It's a ghost,' he whispered. Then, 'It's a *ghost*,' he yelled. He dropped his ball, and himself bounced back down the stairs, nearly knocking over poor Mrs Bonella, who was carrying a bucket of peeled potatoes from the kitchen to the front shop. 'A ghost,' he howled, bolting past her, and clawing at the door to get out.

'What on earth is the matter with that child?' demanded the Ghost, dropping a stitch in his annoyance. 'Now see what he's made me do! Anyone would think he had never seen a ghost before.'

Tim had gone after Stephen, and caught up with him in the lane at the side of the shop. Stephen was trembling, and under the warm gold of his skin he had gone quite pale. Tim grabbed him, and pinned him against the wall.

'Listen, you daft idiot,' he said urgently. 'It's all right. He's harmless. Just some old ghost. We met him last night, and he's okay, honestly.'

'He's an evil spirit,' whimpered Stephen.

'No, he's not,' said Tim patiently. 'He's a conceited twit, but he's not evil. Come and meet him.'

'I daren't. He's—'

'He's not. Oh, come on, Steve. How can anyone be scared of a ghost who knits?'

Although there was no logic in it, this seemed to calm Stephen. 'As long as I don't have to shake

hands with him,' he said, as, clinging to Tim's sleeve, he came indoors again.

'Feeling better?' asked Mrs Bonella, passing by with the bucket.

'He's fine,' said Tim firmly.

'One day,' said Mrs Bonella self-pityingly, 'I'll go where it's quiet.'

Upstairs, the Ghost had picked up his stitch, and recovered his temper. He was telling Dorothy about a brilliant trick he had once done in the pantomime *Aladdin*, which had ended with Pussy Katz appearing out of a bottle. When the two boys reappeared, he was all graciousness.

'I'm delighted to meet you,' he said when Stephen, hands firmly in pockets, was introduced.

31

'These charming young people are going to help me find my magic wand. Perhaps you can assist.'

The three children sat down on the couch, and watched as the Ghost leisurely finished his row, rolled up his wool, and put his knitting tidily away in his bag. 'I like knitting,' he said. 'And tapestry work. Good for my nerves.'

'My mum likes knitting,' said Stephen, daring for the first time to speak directly to the Ghost. His colour was back to normal, and he had stopped shaking, but his eyes were still very round. 'When she can find the time.'

Tim, meanwhile, had remembered a question which had occurred to him that morning in school. 'Mr Porrex,' he said, 'I was wondering. If you lost your magic wand in 1900, why has it taken you so long to come back to look for it? I mean, why didn't you come back in 1901? You'd have had a better chance of finding it, it seems to me.'

The Ghost turned his head, and gave Tim a pale, sad look with a hint of horror in it, which made Tim shiver. Too late, it reminded him of the Ghost's certainty, the previous evening, that there were no angels in hell. 'I was otherwise occupied in 1901,' he said coldly, 'and for a long time after that. I have only recently become free to attend to my own affairs. You should mind your own business.'

Tim agreed, and hastily changed the subject. 'It was Stephen's mum's restaurant the Phantoms raided last night,' he told the Ghost. 'Any trouble, Steve?'

Stephen shrugged his narrow shoulders. 'Just the usual,' he said. 'The fat one, Jake, said they'd break up the dining-room if Mum didn't give them each a free chow-mein, and the spotty one they call Mac-the-Knife kicked a chair about, to let her see they meant business.'

'So your mum gave them the chow-meins,' said Tim, depressed. 'It's the only thing to do. My mum says it's cheap at the price, if it avoids big trouble.'

Stephen scowled. 'They pick on us because we're Chinese,' he said angrily.

Dorothy patted him sympathetically on the knee. 'No, they don't,' she said kindly. 'They pick on us too. They call us Eyeties, and say rude things about our ice-cream. Our family's lived in Scotland for fifty years, and we don't even speak Italian.'

'They call us worse than that,' said Stephen bitterly. 'And they write on our walls, saying that we should go home. But this is home. Alice and I were born here.'

Tim shook his head. 'I don't think it has anything to do with that,' he said. 'I think they're just bully-boys who pick on anybody they think can't hit back. The Camerons at the Posh Potato and the McNabbs at the pub have awful trouble, and they're as Scottish as you can get. Mr

33

McNabb's even written to our Member of Parliament, complaining that the police turn a blind eye.'

There was a glum silence while they all contemplated the wickedness of the Phantoms. But then a gleam came into Dorothy's eye.

'Do you know what I think?' she said. 'I think these Phantoms need a big, horrible fright. You know? The fright of their lives,' she added, looking meaningfully at the Ghost.

For a moment, the two boys looked blank, but then their faces brightened.

'Oh, yes,' breathed Stephen, catching on. 'Oh, Mr Great Porridge—'

'Porrex,' snapped the Ghost.

'That's what I said. Oh, Mr Porridge, would you help us?'

'Please,' begged Dorothy, winsomely.

The Ghost looked in alarm at their pleading faces. 'Now look here,' he said, suddenly edgy. 'I didn't come here to set the world to rights, you know. You need some do-gooding busybody of a ghost for that. I could put you in touch with Florence Nightingale. She'd give them a good fright, would old Flo. She certainly frightens me. But I'm a private ghost, here on private business, to find my magic wand. I don't want to get mixed up in other people's affairs.'

Their reproachful eyes obviously bothered him, but it wasn't until Tim said dismissively, 'Please

34

yourself, then. I don't suppose you'd be much good at frightening people anyway,' that he took the bait, and reacted.

'Young man,' he said, lowering his voice ominously, 'do not forget that I am The Great Porrex, master of a thousand magical feats. In my time, I have terrified the highest and the lowest in the land. But—' Suddenly his voice changed. He threw up his long hands, and went on in the tone of one who has decided to come clean. 'Without my wand, my powers are very limited. I daresay I could tuck my head underneath my arm, and float around saying, "Woo – woo – woo-oo-oo." But that wouldn't scare proper gangsters a bit. And the kind of wholesale terror you have in mind is, frankly, beyond me.'

It was not like him to be so modest, but he sounded so sincere that nobody noticed the crafty expression which had appeared on his face.

'That's it, then,' said Dorothy, and all the children sighed sadly.

'Not necessarily,' said the Ghost quickly. 'But you do now see the importance of finding my wand, don't you? I'll tell you what. We'll strike a bargain. If you manage to find my wand, I shall repay you by frightening these disgraceful youths clean out of Baltic Street, and out of your eating-houses for ever. But remember, please. *It will only be possible after you have found my magic wand.*'

4 In the Park

During the next few days, the Ghost made himself completely at home in the Bonellas' living-room. He appeared and disappeared at all hours, as if he owned the place. He was usually there when the children came home from school, watching television, which he loved, in the company of the unseeing Mrs Bonella. He had finished knitting his luminous green scarf, and was now working on a tapestry picture of Glamis Castle, inspired by his admiration for Mrs Bonella's picture of the Castle at Edinburgh.

'Though I prefer Glamis myself,' he told Dorothy. 'The most haunted castle in Scotland, you know. I'm going up there to a Ghosts' Convention at Hallowe'en.'

'Where did you get your tapestry kit?' asked Dorothy. Although, after Tim's rebuff, she knew better than to ask questions about where the Ghost had been for the last ninety years, she was curious about the details of his private life, such as where he slept, and if he ever fancied a Kentucky Fried Chicken, and whether he went to the lavatory. He was usually cagey in his replies, but he answered this question readily enough.

'In a little shop on the other side. Spooky Wools, it's called. Everything for the discerning craftsghost. I get my knitting yarn there as well,' he told her, as he threaded his bodkin, and put in another shimmering stitch.

The Ghost watched a lot of television in the evenings, too, but usually alone. As soon as homework and tea were over, Tim and Dorothy put on old clothes, and slipped out to rendezvous with Stephen. Looking for the Ghost's magic wand was now an urgent, if unrewarding task, and they felt

they must get on with it, before the long, late autumn nights arrived.

There seemed little they could do, except to go over, as carefully as they could, all the ground which they thought the Baltic Theatre might have covered. Apart from the basements of the Tartan Parrot and the other shops in Baltic Street, which seemed unlikely hunting-ground, this comprised a huge area of overgrown, derelict land lying between the back premises of the Baltic Street shops, and those of the tenements in Salamander Row.

Although they found in the rough, dusty grass, traces of foundations which must have been those of the old theatre, it was impossible to know where the stage had been. And searching in the open for a short wooden stick which had been dropped inside a vanished building nearly a century ago, was, they knew in their hearts, ridiculous.

Yet what else could they do? On Thursday, the Phantoms had extorted six chicken suppers from Mrs Bonella, and Tim and Dorothy had had the distressing task of trying to comfort their mother in floods of tears. Mr Bonella was in the Merchant Navy, and didn't come home very often. Tim took very seriously his job of looking after his mother.

By Friday night the children were fed up, and not best pleased with the Ghost, but when they went upstairs to tell him so, he had disappeared. On Saturday morning they felt too disheartened to search any further, so, after they had been to the supermarket, and finished their weekend chores, they took Stephen's four-year-old sister Alice to the park to play. But they could talk about nothing but The Great Porrex and his wand, for all that the subject was getting on their nerves.

'Anyway, I'm sceptical,' said Tim.

They had got tired of pushing fat Alice on a swing, and were feeding lumps of stale bread to some tatty brown ducks who quacked and paddled buoyantly in a tatty pond. Dorothy thought they were clever ducks because, faced with a choice of soggy bread, soggy cigarette-packets and soggy sweet-papers, they picked out the bread every time. Alice quacked along with them, and had to be prevented every few minutes from joining them in the water.

'What's sceptical?' asked Stephen.

'It means,' replied Tim, 'that I think The Great Porridge is having us on. Everybody knows these magic wands are just a con-trick — they don't actually have any power. He said himself that he conjured up the ghost at the Tivoli Music Hall with a mirror, and he's always boasting about his tricks and illusions.'

'You mean, he could sort out the Phantoms without a wand, if he really wanted to?' said Dorothy, grabbing Alice by the seat of her trousers.

'We don't even know *that*,' pointed out Tim.

'There's absolutely no proof he can do anything at all, except boast his head off, and knit scarves. Any fool can knit.' Dorothy disagreed with this, but decided to let it pass. To have an argument with Tim on the edge of a pond was asking for trouble.

Stephen said, 'I see what you mean, Tim. He may have no power at all, and the bargain he made with us could just be to save his face. He probably knows ruddy fine we'll never find the wand.'

'He can go through walls,' put in Dorothy. 'Perhaps being a ghost gives him special powers.'

'Then he'll have to prove it,' said Tim, as he tossed the last pellet of bread into the midst of the ducks. 'Before we waste any more time poking about among the thistles, I vote we ask for a demonstration. Something to prove he could keep his side of the bargain, and isn't just taking us for a ride.'

They all agreed that this would be prudent. But Dorothy, who was no fool, pointed out that the Ghost must have some good reason for wanting his wand back.

'If it's just a useless wooden stick, like you say,' she said, 'why on earth has he bothered to come back to look for it after ninety years?' It was a good question, but the boys paid no attention. They were ten and a half, and she was only eight, and they never listened to a word she said.

The children thought they would have to wait until evening for an opportunity to challenge the Ghost, when he turned up to watch The Paul Daniels Magic Show, but as they returned through the Botanic Garden, they saw him sitting on a bench under a palm-tree. He was wearing his luminous green scarf, and busily working on his tapestry of Glamis Castle. They went and joined him.

'Battleship grey, with purple thunderclouds for the sky, don't you think?' he asked Dorothy, showing her the half-finished tapestry. 'And lime-green for the forked lightning? That isn't in the pattern – just a clever personal touch,' he added, with a modest air.

'Very pretty,' said Dorothy, untruthfully.

'Any news of my wand?' queried the Ghost, brightly.

'Listen!' said Tim, sharply. He took a poor view of chaps embroidering, although he and Stephen had to do sewing at school now, while the girls went to woodwork. 'We've been thinking – about your wand.'

'Thinking isn't enough,' said the Ghost smugly. 'Action's what's required.'

'Exactly,' agreed Tim. 'That's what we were thinking about you.'

The Ghost pricked his finger.

'Ouch!' he said. Then, 'What were you thinking about me exactly?'

'That we need some action,' said Tim, resisting the temptation to add, 'other than embroidery'. 'Suppose we do find your wand. What proof do we have that you can terrify the Phantoms? We've never even seen you doing a card-trick. If we're to spend more of our valuable time scraping about in muck, looking for your wand, we want – well, a small demonstration of your powers. Just to encourage us, you know.'

Stephen and Dorothy held their breath, but, surprisingly, no explosion of outrage came from the Ghost. He folded up his tapestry, and said, 'Well, why not?'

'Why not what?' Stephen asked.

'Why not give you a demonstration?' said the Ghost. 'It's devilish impertinence on your part to demand it, but – well, to tell the truth, I'm getting bored. Upon whom would you like me to demonstrate? Not a phoney Phantom, remember, because that would breach our agreement. Have you a lesser enemy?'

Tim and Stephen looked at each other, and smiled wickedly. Then they told the Ghost a name.

'Very well,' said the Ghost. 'You may expect a small, free demonstration soon. Meanwhile, I'm going to play on the swings.'

5   A Day at School

Tim and Stephen didn't hate Harbour Green School because it was a grimy old red sandstone building, squashed between the decaying Estonia Docks and the Asda supermarket. They didn't hate its black asphalt playground, with its prison fence of spiky railings, or the corridors lined with shiny white tiles, like a hospital. They even liked the headmaster, Mr Tweedie, who coached the school football team, and saw no good reason why his lads shouldn't get a fixture with the Queen's Academy. And the teachers, with one exception, were just the usual mix of sweet and sour, baggy and stringy, smooth and wizened, ironed and drip-dry, scented and reeking of tobacco. It was the exception which made the boys say, 'We hate school,' when it wasn't really school they hated at all.

The exception was Mr Flyte, who was the teacher of Class 6F. F for Flyte, C for Cardew, and those in 6C thanked their lucky stars. Tim and Stephen were in 6F, and Flyte was the name they had so promptly suggested to the Ghost. For

if ever they had an enemy, Flyte was the man.

When Mr Flyte arrived at school on Monday morning, his usual Monday morning feeling was made worse by the sight of a large crowd of children gathered around the high railings on the other side of the playground. They were laughing uproariously at something he couldn't see. Mr Flyte distrusted laughter, which he regarded as a threat to good order, so, when he had parked his Fiat in the teachers' car park, he hurried across to stop it.

The Ghost had arrived at half-past eight, and was warming up, delighted to have found such an appreciative audience. First, he did a few hand-stands on top of the railings, and, for want of doves, made a few very surprised seagulls fly out of his trousers. Next, he flipped over on his side, and began to weave himself in and out of the railings. When he got to the wall at the end, he did a fancy U-turn, and snaked back again.

The children cheered. The Ghost bowed, and went into a routine where he drew an endless string of pale pink sausages out of his waistcoat pocket. Dorothy noticed that the sausages were as thin and spectral as he was. But what most interested her, and also Stephen and Tim, was that the Ghost's ghostliness did not seem to be observed by anyone but themselves. They listened incredulously to the comments.

'He's advertising the Circus.'

'He'd get those clothes from the Tricks shop up town.'

'You can see through him, though. That's clever.'

'No, it's not. You can get paint that makes you look like that. You see it on the telly all the time.'

Just then Mr Flyte arrived, slightly breathless, and looking like an angry ferret.

'Right then,' he rasped. 'What's going on here? Speak up! What's the joke, eh?'

The children stared at him. It seemed an unnecessary question, when the cause of their amusement was sitting on a spike with his legs tied in a reef-knot, making funny faces and spinning himself like a top. But it was well known that old Flytie could never see a joke.

'Come on, then,' he barked. 'I'm waiting! What's so funny?' He spotted a face to which he could put a name. 'You there – Robert Smythe!'

'Well, it's him,' said Robert Smythe uncertainly. 'That man, sir.'

'What man? I don't see any man.' This was typical Flyte. The children sighed and shuffled, and waited for Robert Smythe to be given a punishment. Fortunately, at that moment, the bell rang.

Mr Flyte did not have a good morning. His was probably the last primary school class in the United Kingdom where you could hear a pin drop most of the time. Even the tough guys from Harbour Lane were terrified of Flyte, whose air of menace could have taught the Phantoms a thing or two. But today was different. The class was restless, almost giggly, and Mr Flyte was uneasily aware that he was not, as usual, the centre of nervous attention. If he had been a fanciful man, he would have suspected that his pupils were distracted by another presence in the room.

There was another presence in the room, all right. The Ghost had come indoors at the end of the 6F line, and now he was sitting at the desk of an absent pupil, doing his tapestry work. He kept winking broadly at Tim and Stephen, who did their best to ignore him.

The other children were confused. They couldn't understand why Mr Flyte didn't roar at the stranger, and tell him to get out of the room. Then they began to wonder whether the Ghost might be a School Inspector – if you could imagine a School Inspector who spun round on his bottom on the end of a spike, pulled sausages out of his pocket, and did his sewing when he should have been asking you questions about your Science projects. This idea was abandoned when the Ghost pinged some pieces of chalk at Mr Flyte while he was putting sums on the blackboard. There was an awful rumpus, because Mr Flyte was the only person in the room with a licence to ping chalk. Then the children went back to supposing that the Ghost was from the Circus, and admiring his cheek.

After morning break, the Ghost accompanied 6F to the gym, where he showed off like mad, doing dare-devil stunts on the ropes and wall-bars, and reducing the class to hysterics. Miss Hooke said they were all as high as kites, and she couldn't understand it, so she sent them back early to Mr Flyte. On the stairs, the Ghost shimmered past Tim and Stephen, whispering, 'Luncheon time for my demonstration, chaps. I'm going to the Zoo in the afternoon.'

'I don't know that this was a good idea, Tim,' Stephen said.

Mr Flyte was on lunch-duty on Mondays, which meant that, instead of drinking coffee and reading the *Dundee Courier* in the staff-room, he had to stalk up and down the dining-room, direct-ing traffic, bawling for silence, and complaining about the children's table manners. Or at least, that was what he thought he had to do. He hated it, although not more than the children eating lunch did. And today was even worse than usual, because his head ached, and every dropped spoon made him wince. Mr Flyte had become aware that someone, somehow, was making a fool of him, and that made him feel very insecure.

The Ghost joined the queue for the self-service counter, squeezing himself in between Dorothy and Stephen.

'You need sixty pence if you're eating,' Dorothy told him.

'I'm not eating,' replied the Ghost. 'I need some custard for my act.' Stephen shuddered, but Dorothy, who did not have to face Mr Flyte in the afternoon, beamed enthusiastically. 'Great stuff,' she said.

When the Ghost reached the food, he helped himself to a large baked potato and a plate of custard and stewed apple. Then he lifted the tray, and swayed across the dining-room, holding it up on his outstretched fingers, like a waiter. The children, who had got used to the presence of the funny man from the Circus, and had decided that he must be a friend of Mr Tweedie's, went on with their lunch. They were hungry, and there would be plenty of time for more entertainment when they had finished eating. Only Mr Flyte saw the tray, to his eyes unattached to any hand, floating across the room. He put his fingers over his eyes, peeped between them fearfully, and said to himself, 'George, you've been overworking.'

But before he could decide what to do, a baked potato bounced off the tray, and hurtled past him, narrowly missing his right ear. Robert Smythe put up his hand and caught it. He squawked, 'Ow, it's hot!' and tossed it to Tim Bonella. Before Mr Flyte could gather enough breath to howl for order, other potatoes were flying through the air, and Mr Flyte's worst nightmare was realised. Children were enjoying themselves, and he was powerless to stop them.

'Sit down,' he roared into the hubbub. 'Sit down and sit up, or I'll – I'll – I'll—' Nobody paid any attention.

It was the Ghost who blew the whistle on the game. Raising the tray high above his head, he made his mouth into a circle, puffed out his cheeks, and blew. A long, piercing whistle was followed by a howling wind, which whooshed through the dining-room, whipping a snowstorm of paper napkins into the air, billowing out the curtains, and making Mr Flyte's thin gingery hair stand right up on end. The bowl of custard left the Ghost's tray at speed, and came straight towards him. He saw it coming in time, and

ducked; the custard flew past him and plastered itself on the wall. But just as Mr Flyte thought he was safe, and was opening his mouth to yell, 'Who did that?' the Ghost decided to reveal himself. Raising his arms, he writhed and wiggled transparently before the horrified teacher, showing the whites of his eyes, and yowling, 'Woo – woo – woo – oo – oo!' Then he blew the rudest of raspberries, and flicked himself off like a television.

With popping eyes, Mr Flyte staggered backwards, lost his balance, and sat down. A table broke his fall, but on the table, where it made contact with his bottom, there happened to be another plate of stewed apple and custard. When he stood up, the mess on his trousers had to be seen to be believed. Silence fell at last.

At the beginning of afternoon school, Mr Tweedie came to Class 6F, and announced that Mr Flyte had gone home with a headache. He did not mention that he also needed to change his trousers.

'Those of you with a parent at home may go,' he said. 'The rest must stay in the playground until half-past three.'

The Ghost was waiting for Tim and Stephen at the corner of Baltic Street. He was looking very pleased with himself.

'Well?' he said.

'You went a bit far, didn't you?' said Tim

reproachfully.

Not surprisingly, the Ghost was peeved. 'It was you who wanted a demonstration,' he pointed out huffily. 'Anyway, by this evening he'll have decided that I was nothing but a bad dream.'

'So we'll get the blame tomorrow,' said Stephen gloomily.

'All pleasure has to be paid for,' said the Ghost. 'I'm off to the Zoo.'

6   At the Circus

'At least we do know now that Porridge can put on a show,' said Stephen on Tuesday evening, while they were exploring another stretch of stale, thistle-sharp wasteland behind the Tartan Parrot. 'He certainly put the wind up old Flytie.' They all grinned.

Mr Flyte had been back in school that morning, in his second-best suit, looking pale and not at all his usual snappy self. Contrary to expectation, he had wreaked no terrible revenge for his humiliation the previous day. No mention of the Ghost's visitation had been made, but the memory of it lay between Mr Flyte and Class 6F. Although he had dismissed his sighting of the Ghost as a headachy fancy, he knew that they knew that he had sat down in a bowl of custard. And that had changed, for the time being, the balance of power. *He* was nervous of *them*.

'We also know,' Dorothy pointed out, 'that he can put on a show without his wand. So why is he so keen to get it back?'

She asked this question again because it seemed

important to her, but once again the boys ignored it.

'The only thing that matters is that he won't sort out the Phantoms until we find it,' said Tim, heaving over a huge stone, and looking disgustedly at the slugs crawling on its underside. 'And I don't think we're going to find it.'

It was the first time that one of them had put this fear into words, and Stephen and Dorothy looked at Tim anxiously. Mrs Cheng had had another visit from the Phantoms on Sunday evening, and things were getting desperate. By the time the police, summoned by Mr McNabb at the pub, had eventually arrived, the Phantoms had gobbled their free supper, mounted their motorbikes, and were far away.

'But we must go on looking,' said Stephen, with angry tears in his eyes. Like Mrs Bonella, his mother was on her own, because his father was working in Hong Kong. 'You aren't going to give up, are you, Tim?'

Tim glanced at him, then glanced away quickly. 'No,' he said. 'Now come on. We'd better shift this pile of tin cans. I suppose it's just possible.' They went to work again, feeling dispirited.

The Ghost had been reclining in his chair in the living-room, watching Double Your Money. When it was finished, he flitted out into the twilight to see how the searchers were getting on. He was wearing the aura of phosphorescence

which he assumed at nightfall, and of which he was very proud. He wafted across the grass, looking eerie.

'Any news of my wand?' he asked brightly, settling down elegantly on a lump of masonry.

'No,' said Tim surlily, straightening his aching back. 'There's not much chance in all this, is there?'

'Oh, I don't know,' responded the Ghost cheerfully. 'I'm sure there are lots of stones still unturned. But don't stay out and catch a chill in the night air, will you? You can look again tomorrow evening.'

It would have been better to have kept quiet,

but one always realises that too late. Dorothy spoke without thinking. 'Oh, we can't look tomorrow evening,' she told the Ghost. 'We're going to the Circus in the park. Mrs Cheng's got tickets for us. It's Stephen's birthday treat.'

The Ghost glowed. 'How delightful,' he said enthusiastically. 'I haven't been to the Circus since Barnum's in 1871. I shall look forward to it. When do we meet?'

They managed not to groan.

'Six o'clock,' said Stephen feebly.

The gaily flagpoled Big Top, which looked from the outside like an enormous moulded blanc-mange, felt chilly inside, its smell a mixture of damp grass, canvas and animals' spoor. Tim, Stephen and Dorothy clambered up steep wooden steps, and slid along the bench to their seats, M17, M18, and M19. Dorothy looked fearfully under the bench, contemplating the drop through dark nothingness to the ground far below.

'Don't look,' advised Tim, opening the pro-gramme which Stephen had bought, and peering at it in the dim light. 'You're perfectly safe, isn't she, Mr Porrex?'

'I used to suffer badly from vertigo,' said the Ghost, who had settled himself into seat M20. 'In view of the manner of my death, I suppose that might seem prophetic. Now, of course, I don't mind at all. But yes – you're quite safe, Dorothy.

Just watch the show, my dear, and don't keep looking through your knees.'

The children wondered what would happen if someone arrived with the ticket for seat M20. Would the Ghost move, or would they sit on his knee without knowing he was there? It might have been interesting, but they did not find out. The Circus had already been in the park for four days, the nights were growing colder, and when the lights went up in the ring for the start of the performance, the tent was only two-thirds full. No one came to challenge the Ghost, and as the Great Parade of the Animals began, he crossed his legs, folded his arms, and smiled happily. 'I *am* glad you invited me,' he enthused. 'This really *is* what I call fun!'

'Just as long as he behaves,' muttered Tim. But Stephen spread his thin hands fatalistically, and said, 'Too late to worry now.'

BOOM-BOOM, TITTY-TITTY, BOOM-BOOM, BOOM-BOOM! trumpeted the Circus Band, squashed in a little red box above the red-curtained entrance to the ring. COME TO THE CIRCUS, THE GREATEST SHOW ON EARTH! Well, it was hardly that, but it was different from the telly, and, despite the chilly draughts and the hard seats, all the spectators were out to enjoy themselves, none more so than the Ghost.

He laughed uproariously at the clowns, in their

bowler hats and baggy trousers, nearly sliding off his seat with mirth when their leader, Mojo, was squirted with water by an elephant tasselled like an outsize lampshade. He applauded wildly the little dogs in frilly collars who walked on their hind legs and jumped through hoops. He called encouragement to an anxious-looking Indian lady, who was trying to coax a bored python into a more tricksy frame of mind. He ooh-ed and ah-ed with delight at the Flying Swingeroos, leaping and somersaulting on the high trapeze.

'I wouldn't mind having a go at that,' he said longingly. 'I wonder if they have a vacancy for a trainee?'

At the interval, he went off by himself to look at the Menagerie, while Tim, Stephen and Dorothy ate ice-cream, and remarked to each other that all was going pretty well. The children in the audience, who could see him, had their attention elsewhere, and the adults, who might have thought him a bit over the top, fortunately couldn't see him at all.

'No call for a demonstration tonight,' said Tim thankfully. He had completely forgotten that he was the one who had goaded the Ghost into demonstrating, and was now taking a very prim attitude to the Ghost's hanky-panky at school.

'There won't be any trouble,' said Dorothy soothingly. 'He's just like the rest of us, having a good night out.'

Only, of course, he was not like the rest of them.

The first act after the interval was The Intrepid Monsieur Smee and his Ferocious Lions, but for the first time the Ghost showed no interest. As Monsieur Smee, a small, mustachioed man in green satin trousers, cracked a whip inside a cage, and two mothy, thin-faced lions hopped wearily on and off stools, the Ghost sighed and tutted impatiently.

'Any self-respecting lions,' he remarked to Stephen, 'would eat him. But they can't. They haven't got any teeth.'

'How d'you know?' asked Stephen, shocked.

'When I was looking at them in the Menagerie,' replied the Ghost, 'they happened to yawn.'

His boredom was not, however, to last long. When the lions were towed away to, presumably, a sloppy supper, the Band played a fanfare, and into the ring ran a girl wearing a top hat, black velvet jacket and spangled tights. She was followed by a page-boy, carrying a small table with a black and silver chest on top. With much swaggering, and waving, and pouting her scarlet lips, the girl opened the chest, took out a black box, opened it and held it up to the audience. When she had convinced everyone that it was empty, she closed it, twirled it, and opened it again. Out flew five white doves, which perched on a pole held by her boy assistant. Carefully, he carried them away. The girl then went into a

60

standard magician's routine, spinning plates, bringing a rabbit out of her top hat, and juggling with balls which, one by one, seemed to disappear into the air.

The children really expected the Ghost to look disdainfully on this performance. Surely this was elementary stuff to The Great Porrex. But when they glanced along at him, they saw that he had stopped fidgeting, and had become very attentive indeed. This made them nervous, without exactly knowing why, but nothing happened until the girl, during a patter of applause for her juggling, took from the chest a gold and silver banded wand. She held it up, smiled widely, and mouthed into a microphone, 'Ladies and gentlemen! For my final feat of magic this evening, I am going to use this very powerful magic wand. I am going to ask my assistant, Billy—'

But Tim, Dorothy and Stephen never heard what she was going to ask her assistant, Billy. Their attention was now riveted on the Ghost, who had slid forward onto the edge of his seat, and was trembling violently.

'Timothy!' he commanded. 'Let me see the programme!'

Tim pushed it in front of him, and the Ghost squinted at it in the dim light.

'I knew it,' he roared. 'Hell's fangs! It's Pussy Katz, and that's my wand!'

Tim looked down at the programme. 'Item 22,'

he read aloud. 'Magic for You. Miss Kitty Katz.'

'It can't be,' said Dorothy. 'Mr Porrex—'

But it was too late. Rising from his seat, the Ghost launched himself like a rocket over the heads of the people sitting in rows A to L. Leading with his head, he shot torpedo-like around the ring, bore down upon the unfortunate Miss Kitty Katz, and snatched the wand out of her hand. He made her see him – no doubt about that. Abandoning Billy and the apparatus of her act, she ran out of the ring, screaming blue murder. The children in the audience cheered and clapped like mad.

'It's the man who came to school!'

'The one who made Flytie sit down in the custard!'

'I said he was from the Circus!'

'Hey, mister! Do another trick!'

The Ghost paid no attention. He was holding up the wand in front of him, picking and scratching at it, peering at it with eyes narrowed to slits. Tim and Stephen had their heads in their hands, but Dorothy, who was watching closely, found this interesting. She was beginning to have her own ideas about why the Ghost was so keen to recover his long-lost wand.

And there was something else. She had been standing behind the Ghost in the dining-room queue on Monday, and she had observed that when he seemed to pick up the tray, the potato, and the bowl of pudding, he did not actually touch these things. He seemed to attract them to him, like a magnet, but there was always a millimetre or so of air between them and his hands. This had made her wonder what would happen if the Ghost actually tried to pick up something real. The answer, she now realised, was that what he picked up was the ghost of the thing itself. While the Ghost held the wand he had snatched from the hand of Miss Kitty Katz, another wand lay in the sawdust of the ring, with the top hat, the overturned table, and the box of tricks.

Dorothy watched the Ghost realising that he had made a mistake. Petulantly, he threw the wand from him. It dropped down and merged into the one lying on the ground. There was more cheering from the children around the ring, more shouts of, 'Go on, mister! Fly again! Do the trick with the sausages you did at school!'

So, unable to resist the temptation to show off, the Ghost put his disappointment behind him, and complied.

While Billy ran around, tidying away the magic apparatus of the unfortunate Miss Katz, the Ghost levitated and flew around the ring, turning himself green, orange and purple by turns, and showering the audience with sparks which only the children could see. They ducked and screamed, while the adults wondered what on

earth was the matter with Miss Katz, and remarked that circuses overexcited children.

The Ghost was now into the swing of things. Crackling electrically, he shot up to the high wire, where he wobbled to and fro, falling off to gasps of horror, regaining his balance to whoops of relief. He had a go on the trapeze, proving that he would not be a trainee for long. Then he wrote 'I Am The Greatest' in the air, with a long ribbon of smoke which seemed to issue from his left ear. When the dancing ponies entered, he wafted down and performed with them, standing on one leg on one pony's back, doing a handstand on the back of another, cartwheeling on the back of a third.

For the rest of the performance he took part in every act, riding elephants, jumping through flaming hoops, out-clowning the clowns. The children, apart from Stephen, Tim and Dorothy, were delirious with admiration, and the circus people, apart from Miss Kitty Katz, who was lying down in her caravan, thought this was the most marvellous audience they had ever had in their lives. The Ringmaster did not, of course, call on the Ghost to take a bow, so he took one anyway, and gave himself several extra curtain-calls.

'What a wonderful evening,' said the Ghost exultantly, as they left the dimly luminous Big Top behind them, and made their way through the dark park towards the hard brightness of the night streets. 'Pity about my wand, though. Do you know, it was *exactly* like mine – gold and silver stripes, with a little gold knob on top.'

'Then how do you know it wasn't yours,' asked Tim, 'if it was *exactly* the same?'

The Ghost turned cagey. 'It didn't feel right. But you can't blame me for investigating, Timothy,' he added. 'That girl was the spit of Pussy. She must be a great-granddaughter, I suppose. I wonder if I should go and have another chat with her?'

'Only if you want to scare her to death. And don't call me Timothy,' said Tim.

7   Poor Pussy

At the beginning of October, the dusty green leaves of the park trees crackled into gold. The Ghost finished his tapestry of Glamis Castle, and began to knit himself a pair of purple mittens for the frosty days ahead. The children had a week's half-term holiday from school, and the Ghost suggested that they ought to spend it searching seriously for his wand.

'No can do,' said Tim firmly, when he had recovered from the cheek of it. 'Mrs Cheng is closing the Golden Dragon for a week, and Steve and I are going to paint the dining-room. It will be a big job, so we'll have no time for wand-hunting. Of course, you could go out and do a bit of stone-shifting yourself. The fresh air would do you good.'

'In my condition?' protested the Ghost indignantly. 'I never heard of such a thing!'

Hastily, Dorothy declared that she wouldn't be available either. Her friend Hannah had found a trunk full of old clothes in her attic, and she and Dorothy planned to spend their holiday dressing up, putting on make-up, and acting plays.

The Ghost was so offended by what he called their heartless lack of co-operation that he disappeared for several days. But then one evening, towards the end of the holiday week, he turned up suddenly in the Bonellas' living-room, settling into his favourite chair as if nothing at all had happened. So he was present when Stephen arrived, painty and wide-eyed, to announce that the Portly Puss pet shop had been broken into the previous night. The finger of suspicion pointed, as usual, at the Phantoms.

'My mum met Mrs Peebles from the Portly Puss at the supermarket,' said Stephen, dropping breathlessly onto the couch, 'and Mrs Peebles told her all about it. The Phantoms broke in at midnight through a window at the back of the shop. They let all the animals except the python out, and threw pet-food and sawdust all over the place. The animals were so scared that they pee-ed and pooped everywhere. Mrs Peebles says she never saw such a mess in her life.'

'It's cruelty,' said Dorothy, upset. 'They should get in the Royal Scottish Society for the Prevention of Cruelty to Animals.'

'Oh, never mind that,' said Tim impatiently. 'Did they get the police, Steve? Were the Phantoms caught?' Dolefully, Stephen shook his black head.

'No chance,' he said. 'About half-past twelve,

68

Mr Peebles was woken up by all the barking and yowling and chattering downstairs, but when he went down, the Phantoms were gone. He 'phoned the police, but he might as well not have bothered. The usual story,' concluded Stephen bitterly.

'I suppose,' put in the Ghost, who had finished knitting his mittens, and was embroidering yellow daisies on the backs, 'there is some actual proof that these Phantoms—' he winced as he uttered the word '—were responsible?'

Stephen shook his head again. 'The police went to their houses to interview the Phantoms,' he told the Ghost. 'But their mums and dads swore they'd been at home all evening, and had been tucked up in bed with their teddy-bears since half-past nine. If you could believe that, you could believe anything!'

'So there is no proof,' the Ghost sighed.

'Proof! Who needs proof?' burst out Stephen angrily. 'It's obvious, isn't it? Big Pinky Mackintosh has scratches all over his ugly mug, and everyone knows it's a revenge attack because Mr Peebles refused to give Mac-the-Knife a free kitten for his granny's birthday.'

'Even so, we need proof,' insisted the Ghost.

'Talking of kittens,' said Dorothy anxiously, 'are the animals all right, Stephen?'

'Most of them,' Stephen told her. 'If the Phantoms hadn't been too cowardly to let the python out, there might have been terrible casualties. As

69

it was, two canaries died of fright, and a lot of goldfish ended up inside cats. A hamster fell into a fish-tank and drowned, and a Persian kitten is missing. Called Soo Moo Poo Choo, but answers to Charlie.'

'And guess where Soo Moo Poo Choo is eating his Catt-o-meat today,' said Tim grimly. 'In Mac-the-Knife's granny's kitchen, that's where.'

The Ghost nodded. 'It is indeed a wicked world,' he observed piously. Then, trying on a finished mitten, he said again, 'We need proof.'

The next afternoon, the two boys finished paint-ing the enormous golden dragon which snaked

exuberantly along Mrs Cheng's dining-room wall. They were delighted with the result, and so was Mrs Cheng.

'Next holiday, we're going to repaint the Bay of Naples,' Stephen said.

That evening, their labours over, the boys decided that they would relax with a game of Trivial Pursuit. The Ghost was casting on a pale mauve sock, but Dorothy said she would like to play, so she and Stephen sat down at the table, while Tim went to his room to fetch the game.

'You ought to be out—' began the Ghost, but Stephen said firmly, 'Not tonight, Mr Porridge. Sorry. We're far too tired.'

'Stephen,' said the Ghost irascibly. 'Not Porridge. Porrex. Watch my lips. P-O-R-R-E-X. How would you like it if I called you Stuffing Choong?'

Stephen laughed. 'I wouldn't mind much,' he said. 'I've been called worse than that. But I'll try to remember.' The Ghost had more to say, but just at that moment Tim reappeared in the doorway, without the game. He looked very cross.

'Right then, you lot,' he said abruptly. 'Who's been messing about in my room? Was it you, Dotty?' Dorothy stared at him in astonishment.

'I never go into your room. You don't allow me,' she said.

'Too right,' snapped Tim. 'Then what about you, Mr Porrex? Have you been playing tricks in my room today?'

71

The expression on the Ghost's face reminded Tim of something he was apt to forget. He was a ghost who had already displayed considerable power, and you really should watch your step.

'Certainly not,' said the Ghost icily. 'How dare you suggest such a thing?'

'Sorry,' said Tim hastily. 'I didn't mean it, honestly. But someone's been in my room. Come and see.'

The Ghost rose majestically, and they all crowded into the narrow passage from which the bedrooms opened. Peering through the door of Tim's, they saw that the bedside lamp had been knocked over, Lego scattered everywhere, and most of the books on the bookshelf tipped onto the floor. The duvet was hanging off the bed, and one of the yellow curtains had been pulled from its rail.

'Is anything missing, Tim?' asked Stephen, puzzled.

'I don't think so,' replied Tim, 'although I haven't looked carefully. It just looks like vandalism to me.'

'For which you though *I* might be responsible,' sniffed the Ghost, affronted again.

'I have said I'm sorry,' replied Tim.

'So you should be. Do you always keep your window wide open?' enquired the Ghost.

'It's Mum. She believes in fresh air,' said Tim, shivering.

'Do you think it's the Phantoms again?' whispered Dorothy in a scared voice.

'No. The mess isn't bad enough,' Tim reassured her. 'Besides, you'd have to be a cat-burglar to get up the outside wall. The Phantoms are so fat on other people's grub, they could hardly climb the stairs.'

The Ghost flitted over to the open window, and stuck out his head. 'I agree,' he said, after he had looked about outside. 'For once, the – ugh – Phantoms are not involved.'

'Then – who?' chorused the children.

The Ghost looked smug. 'Easy,' he responded airily, 'to one whose powers of observation are as highly developed as my own. I have often thought that, if I had not decided to become the world's greatest magician, I might have turned my genius to detection. There was a chap called Sherlock Holmes—'

Not for the first time, the children had to hold back groans.

'Please, do tell us, Mr Porrex,' pleaded Dorothy, shaking her golden curls, and assuming the air of humility which made her flavour of the month with the Ghost.

'Look here, then,' said the Ghost, pointing. 'Scratch marks on the window-sill, a little wee-wee on the floor, long grey hairs on the curtain. What more evidence do you need? The culprit was not a cat-burglar, but a cat.'

The children looked at one another, as under-standing dawned.

'Soo Moo Poo Choo?' suggested Dorothy.

'Answers to Charlie,' Stephen said.

'And for your further interest,' said the Ghost, delighted with himself, 'there is a small cat on the roof of your mother's outhouse. It is mewing faintly, and I don't think it knows how to get down.'

The children rushed to the window, and thrust out their heads, peering into the darkening yard behind the shop. On the other side of the paved alley where the delivery vans backed in, there was a stone-built outhouse where Mrs Bonella kept potatoes, and Tim and Dorothy kept their bicy-cles. Apparently stuck to the sloping, slate roof there could be discerned a small grey furry object which was, as the Ghost said, uttering faint and plaintive mews.

'There's a step-ladder in the back shop,' said Tim, pulling in his head, and the children whizzed off downstairs. The Ghost followed in a slower, more stately fashion.

The next problem, as soon became apparent, was that the step-ladder did not reach the out-house roof. When Tim stood on the top step, his chest was level with the gutter, and he was afraid to lift himself onto the roof with his arms, for fear that the ancient guttering would give way. The kitten was too petrified to retreat, but neither did it respond to Tim's pleas to move towards him.

'Come on, then, Soo Moo Poo Choo! Nice pussy, come and get some Whiskas! There's a good moggy! Oh, shift yourself, you stupid beast, before I throw a pail of water over you!'

The Ghost, without benefit of ladder, levitated, and trod air alongside Tim.

'The trouble with you, Timothy,' he said, 'is that you have no delicacy. You are frightening the poor little creature, who, by the way, seems to have a label of some sort tied round its neck. Now look. I, with my superior power of attraction, shall lure the kitten to the edge of the roof. You must be ready to grab it as soon as it comes within reach. Understood?'

'Understood,' said Tim, realising that this might not be the best time to tell the Ghost that he was a boastful twit. And he had to admit that what the Ghost did next was very clever indeed.

Hovering lightly at the roof's edge, the Ghost began to emit high-pitched and convincing cater-wauls, 'Mi-au-ow! Mi-au-ow! Mi-au-ow-ow-ow!' while at the same time breathing out an odour of fish so strong that it nearly knocked Tim off the ladder. It obliterated completely the vaguely fishy, fatty smell which hung about outside the café, and which had probably attracted the kitten in the first place. Rude, retching noises floated up from Stephen and Dorothy down below, but the kitten found the smell irresistible. Slowly it began to

creep towards the source, its tiny claws scratching on the slates as it slithered precariously down the slope. Just as it was about to tumble over the gutter, Tim shot out his hand and gripped the fur at the back of its neck.

'Right, I've got him,' he said, and descended with the writhing, spitting bundle of furry fury held at arm's length. The kitten knew it had been conned, and didn't like it.

Tim carried it towards the light outside the house door, and there they gathered round to read the message on the dirty white label tied round its neck with a piece of string.

> *'To Grany, wishing yoo a happy birthday*
> *from MacAlister.'*

'Proof,' said the Ghost, with deep satisfaction.

8 Dr Porrex

When Mr and Mrs Peebles received the kitten
back from the children, they took it to the police
station, with the evidence against Mac-the-Knife
still firmly attached. The result was that Mac was
charged with breaking and entering the Portly
Puss pet shop on the night of 13th October, and
stealing one pedigree Persian kitten. His granny,
Mrs McClusker, confirmed that her grandson
MacAlister had indeed given her a bonnie wee
kitten for her birthday, but it had run away in a
huff after she had smacked it for widdling on the
settee. She had no idea where MacAlister had got
the kitten; he was a kind-hearted laddie, always
good to old folk, even if he did shave his head and
put a ring through his nose. To the children's
disappointment and the Ghost's fury, Mac was
not sent off immediately to prison, but was
allowed to swagger about as usual, while awaiting
trial. The police said there was no proof that the
other Phantoms had been involved.

Stephen, Dorothy and Tim each received a five-
pound note and a goldfish from Mr Peebles as a

reward for finding and returning the kitten. The Ghost was a bit miffed by this, pointing out, correctly, that he had done all the work. But he did admit that he had gone beyond the point where an earthly fiver would be much use to him. 'Although some small token of appreciation would have been pleasing,' he sighed.

'You can share the goldfish,' Dorothy told him kindly. But the Ghost said he didn't like goldfish, and would have preferred a mouse.

At Hallowe'en – the very time, as Tim lamented, when having a real ghost around would have been useful – the Ghost was away up north, attending the Ghosts' Convention at Glamis Castle. He reappeared at the end of the first week in November, in a very good mood, and having had a wonderful time.

'A first-rate programme of events,' he told the children enthusiastically, as they gathered round the living-room fire, on the evening of his return. 'Lectures and group discussions in the mornings, counselling sessions and individual therapy in the afternoons, concert parties and visits to local haunts of interest in the evenings, under a full moon. On the last evening we had a wonderful Spooks' Ball, with a ghostly bagpiper brought over specially from the Isle of Skye to play for the reels. I loved every minute of it. The only disappointment was that we had been promised a guest appearance by the Monster of Glamis, but he failed to – er, materialise.'

'Why would a ghost need therapy?' enquired Stephen.

'Problems of readjustment,' explained the Ghost seriously. 'It's a dramatic change of lifestyle, you know, especially if you have been, um, doing time, as most of us have.' This was the nearest he ever got to telling them where he had been since 1900.

Dorothy was looking in fascination at his knitting needles, from which hung down two-thirds of a lacy pink jumper, with a frilly bit round the edge.

'You're not going to wear that, are you?' she asked repressively. She had got used to luminous scarves and tasteless mittens, but there had to be a limit, even for a ghost.

To her surprise, the Ghost simpered, and she could almost have sworn he blushed.

'It isn't for me,' he said coyly. 'I've got a girl-friend. She was in my discussion group at Glamis – the sweetest little wraith you ever saw. Went down on the *Titanic* in 1912.'

'What's her name?' asked Dorothy, while the boys stared at the Ghost in amazement and disgust.

'Aggie,' said the Ghost. 'She's haunting in Aberdeen till Christmas, but we're going on holiday together in the New Year. I assume you'll have found my wand by then,' he added balefully, purling three and knitting two together.

'Here we go again,' muttered Tim, under his breath. Would he never stop rabbiting on about his silly wand? And would the Phantoms ever be defeated?

'It isn't as if he really needs it,' said Tim, when the Ghost had rolled up his knitting, and gone off through the wall to wherever it was he spent the night. 'He's proved over and over again that he can do any number of tricks without it – some of them quite good, you have to admit. That one with the fishy smell was very clever.'

'He's just trying to blackmail us,' said Stephen crossly. 'Unless we find the wand, he won't bomb out the Phantoms for us. That's a kind of black-mail isn't it?'

'I suppose so. But why does he want it so much?' wondered Tim. 'Why come back here looking for it at all, if it's just a worthless piece of wood? And why keep belly-aching on about it now? He hates the Phantoms nearly as much as we do, and he'd like fine to see them skirling down Baltic Street with their tails on fire. So what's stopping him? It just doesn't make sense.'

Dorothy hugged her teddy, and thought how stupid they were. She had a pretty good idea of why the Ghost wanted his wand back. But if Tim and Stephen, the biggest pair of smart-alecs she had ever met, couldn't work it out for themselves, *she* certainly wasn't going to tell them.

Now gales blew from the north, raking the leaves from the trees in the park, and autumn slipped into winter. The children, as well as the Ghost, put on gloves and mufflers, and the long count-down to Christmas began.

The trial of MacAlister McClusker took place the third week in November. He was found guilty, and sentenced to a hundred hours of community service. This meant that he had to spend three evenings a week down at the Old People's Home, carrying trays and terrifying old ladies who weren't used to attendants with shaved heads and rings through their noses. Since Mac finished work when the old ladies went to bed at eight o'clock, he was free in the later part of the evening to pursue his career as a Phantom. So life went on much as usual.

It was not long, however, before the leader of the gang, Big Pinky Mackintosh, incurred the displeasure of the Ghost. This led to an incident which, while far from settling the Phantom problem for good, gave the children much satisfaction. It also kept alive their hopes of better things to come.

The Ghost regarded Tim and Stephen as two impudent squirts, and remarked frequently that he would never have dared to speak to his elders and betters the way they spoke to him. Mrs Bonella and Mrs Cheng had been heard saying the same. But the Ghost was very fond of Dorothy, who was always polite to him, soothing his easily ruffled feelings, and taking an interest in his knitting. Admittedly she was too inquisitive about his private affairs, and recently had been boring him with requests for more smells. But on the whole she was a dear little girl, whose golden curls reminded him of his little sisters, away back in the 1860's. So when, one afternoon, Dorothy came home from school crying because she had been waylaid by Big Pinky Mackintosh and robbed of her Mars Bar, the Ghost was very angry indeed.

'Only a cad would treat a young lady in such a fashion,' he said indignantly, in his old-fashioned way. 'Now don't cry any more, Dorothy. Timothy can buy you another confection out of his five-pound note. And be sure that if I meet Mr Pinky Mackintosh, I shall teach him a lesson – although not to the extent of upsetting our bargain about my wand, of course.'

Two days later, Dorothy had an appointment at the Health Centre to have treatment for a verruca. Mrs Bonella had intended to take her, but the van which brought her supplies of fish had failed to turn up at the right time, and she could not leave the café until it came.

'I'm sorry, my love,' she said to Dorothy, feeling guilty, as she always did when her work as a shopkeeper interfered with her duty as a mother. 'Tim will go with you, won't you, Tim? The appointment's with Dr Fargo at a quarter to four. All you have to do is give your name at the desk, and wait.'

'It doesn't matter, Mum,' said Dorothy, upset by the look in her mother's eyes. 'I'm only going to get more white stuff on the verruca. It's not as if my foot's hanging off.'

'Yet,' said Tim.

They met the Ghost at the end of Baltic Street, peering entranced through the window of an antiques shop.

'My mamma had a tea-caddy like that,' he said, pointing. Then, pleasantly, he added, 'Whither away?'

84

Taking this to mean, 'Where are you going?'
Dorothy replied, 'To the Health Centre, to see Dr
Fargo about my verruca.'

'I'll come,' said the Ghost immediately. 'I've
never been to the Health Centre.' So he strolled
between them down Finland Place. 'But shouldn't
it be the Illness Centre?' he enquired.

The Health, or Illness Centre was a flat white
building tucked in behind the Post Office.

'Dr Stookie or Dr Fargo?' asked the receptionist, peering through her germ-proof glass screen.

'Dr Fargo,' said Dorothy.

'Take a seat in the waiting-room, please,' said
the receptionist, ticking off Dorothy's name in her
notebook.

It was early, and apart from a young woman
with a baby in a pram, the waiting-room was
empty. Dorothy, Tim and the Ghost took three
seats. Tim read a frayed *Beano* from a pile of old
comics on a low table. Dorothy read the posters
on the walls which told you about all the diseases
you could get. The Ghost made faces at the baby,
who could see him. The baby got very excited,
and began to giggle, and wave its cuddly toy.

'Wheesht, Blake,' said its mother, from behind
Woman's Own. But since the baby was laughing,
not roaring, she paid no more attention.

The Ghost called, 'Coochy-coo!' and wiggled
his fingers at the baby, who went into fits of mirth.
For a moment, it was the happiest baby on earth.

Unfortunately, just then Big Pinky Mackintosh walked into the waiting-room, causing the baby to change its tune. It took one look at Pinky, stopped laughing, and started howling at the pitch of its lungs.

Dorothy knew how it felt.

'It's Big Pinky,' she whispered to the Ghost, sliding as far down in her chair as she could without falling off. 'I don't want him to see me. I'm scared.'

The Ghost was staring at Pinky in a mixture of disbelief, astonishment and disgust. He was indeed a fearsome sight to behold, with his shaved head and bristling chin. He had an earful of metal studs, tattoos all over his neck and hands, and a ring through his left nostril. His small blue eyes were watery, and his nose as red as Rudolph's. Pinky had a stinking cold, and apparently no handkerchief.

'Aw, shurrup,' he said threateningly to the baby, who howled the louder. Its mother bounced the pram with her foot, and said, 'Oh, there, there. The laddie won't eat you.'

The Bonellas thought this was a matter of opinion. But before anything too terrible could happen, a disembodied voice crackled over the intercom. 'Mrs Gray. Dr Fargo's room, please.'

The mother got up thankfully, and wheeled the roaring baby towards the door marked, 'Dr Fargo'. Even when the door was closed, the howls could still be heard, smothered but unabated.

'Where's Stookie?' demanded Pinky, clanking the chains on his leather jerkin as he leaned forward to pick up a *Dandy*. 'I don't like being kept waiting.'

Neither Tim nor Dorothy cared to reply to this, but just then the receptionist put her head round the corner of the partition, and said, 'Oh, Mr Mackintosh, I'm so sorry. I'm afraid Dr Stookie has been held up – there's been an accident up at Dockland Cross. He's just 'phoned to say he'll be here in ten minutes. Would you like to wait in his room? If so, do go in.'

She was so polite that Dorothy wondered whether Pinky had ever jumped out on her, and nicked her Mars Bar on the way home.

Pinky lumbered to his feet, and, swearing under his breath, crossed heavily to the door marked, 'Dr Stookie'. There, with his hand on the door-knob, he turned and glowered at the receptionist.

'Is Stookie the wee fat wife with red hair and a moustache?' he demanded abruptly.

The receptionist became dignified. 'The lady doctor,' she replied coldly, 'is Dr Croker. Dr Stookie is a tall, dark gentleman.'

'Well, I hope he can cure colds,' snarled Pinky, disappearing into the consulting-room.

'Oh dear! I do hope Dr Fargo takes me before Dr Stookie arrives,' wailed Dorothy. 'I don't want to walk home in the dark when Pinky's on the loose.'

But the Ghost was smiling, and stroking his black beard. 'I have an idea,' he said. 'Draw closer. I want to whisper.' So they did, and he did, and as they listened, Tim's and Dorothy's eyes grew wider and wider.

'You couldn't,' said Tim. 'I'm sure it's against the law.'

'I am beyond the law,' said the Ghost calmly, 'and the Pinky Mackintoshes of this world hold no terrors for me. I am a tall dark gentleman, and, apart from the fact that I have vowed to teach Mr Mackintosh a lesson, I am sure Dr Stookie would be grateful to me for dealing with someone come to waste his time with a cold in the head. Three drops of tincture of opium in hot water, and an early night – that's the cure for a cold.'

He rose smoothly to his feet, straightened his tie, and walked quite solidly across to Dr Stookie's door, remembering to open it before he went in.

Dorothy and Tim sat in the empty waiting-room, glancing nervously at each other, torn between anxiety and the desire to laugh. For a few tense moments there was absolute silence, since even the baby had calmed down. But then, all of a sudden, there was pandemonium. Even the sound-proofed walls could not muffle the bawling of Pinky Mackintosh. There were thumps and bangs, and the familiar sound of The Great

Porrex going, 'Woo, woo, woo-oo-oo!' Then a lot of explosions like squibs being set off. Suddenly the door burst open, and Pinky emerged like a greyhound out of the trap. Apart from his nose, his face was blanched with terror, and as he fled through the waiting-room, Dorothy and Tim could hear him whimpering, 'Oh, I'm having a nightmare! I'm delirious! I'm ill! Oh, Mummy! Oh, Daddy! Help!'

Dr Porrex did not disclose the details of the treatment he had given Pinky. But when Dorothy came out after seeing Dr Fargo, she found Tim and the Ghost reclining on chairs, with wide grins on their faces. The real Dr Stookie was running round distractedly, squirting a lavender air-freshener, trying in vain to get rid of the most awful stink-bomb smell.

9   At the Christmas Party

During the next fortnight, when the Phantoms raided the restaurants of Baltic Street, only five chow-meins, lamb tikkas or fish suppers were demanded, since Big Pinky Mackintosh was at home in bed, ill.

At the supermarket, Mrs Bonella heard from Mrs Mackintosh, a woman for whom she felt nothing but pity, that Percival – that was Pinky's proper name – had gone to the doctor with a bad cold, and had come home delirious. To his parents' distress, he seemed convinced that Dr Stookie had hung upside-down from the ceiling, gone, 'Woo, woo, woo-oo-oo!' and thrown stink-bombs and exploding sausages around the consulting-room. When Dr Stookie had been called to see him at home, Percival had hidden under the bedclothes, refused to put out his tongue and say, 'Ah-ah', and accused Dr Stookie of being an impostor. Dr Stookie said that Percival had been overworking at the Polytechnic, and must stay quietly in bed for the next ten days.

'It's an ill wind that blows nobody any good,'

said Mrs Bonella to Mrs Cheng, as they walked home together through the frosty dusk. 'No one wants a young man to be ill, goodness knows, but I'll be glad enough to save a fish supper when it's my turn to provide the Phantoms with their evening meal.'

'Yes, indeed,' agreed Mrs Cheng.

Now it was December, and in the first snowfall of the winter, the Ghost went tobogganing with the children on Jubilee Brae, and stared in wonder at the lighted Christmas tree in Baltic Square. But what excited him most was the prospect of the school Christmas party, to which he had not been invited, but which he had every intention of

attending. The boys, fearing another confrontation with Flyte, tried hard to dissuade him.

'It's boring,' said Tim. 'We only go because we have to. 'Pass the Parcel', and 'In and Out the Dusty Bluebells'. And you have to dance with girls. It isn't cool.'

The Ghost said that he remembered 'Pass the Parcel' from parties long ago, and that heat had no effect on him. Tim rolled his eyes at the ceiling. It was a waste of time trying to make the Ghost understand modern speech. He always got it wrong.

'The food's lousy,' warned Stephen. 'Melted ice-cream and sloppy jelly, and stale potato crisps that Flytie gets cheap from the cash and carry.'

The Ghost said that the quality of the food did not concern him.

'But you haven't got a ticket,' burst out Tim in desperation. This was so ridiculous that the Ghost didn't deign to reply.

When he heard that there was ten-pin bowling at the Community Centre the same afternoon, he did briefly waver, and it was Dorothy who made up his mind finally by telling him, indiscreetly, that a conjuror was to appear at the school party.

'After the games, we're having tea,' she informed the Ghost. 'Then a conjuror, and Santa Claus before we go home.'

'That settles it. I'll come,' said the Ghost eagerly. 'I can go ten-pin bowling any old time. I can't resist a conjuror, and I really would hate to disappoint you all.'

It was not the first time that Dorothy had made this mistake, and she had to take a lot of flak from the boys in private. But it was too late. A party with Porrex was inevitable now.

The party took place in the School Hall on the afternoon of Saturday, 19th December. Dressed in their best clothes, Dorothy, Stephen and Tim arrived promptly at two o'clock, joining the other children who were converging on the brightly lit, gaily decorated hall. The atmosphere was fairly subdued. It was generally agreed that this party was not as much fun as the Sunday School Treat, or the Cub and Brownie Revels, where the organisers were merely mums and dads. At this one, the organisers were teachers, and a teacher is a teacher, even on Saturday afternoon. And the Master of Ceremonies was Mr Flyte, whose air of menace was only increased by his wearing a jazzy pullover and a paper hat. There would be no rioting and sliding and falling on the floor here.

Dorothy ran at once to join the other girls who were huddling and squealing at one end of the hall. The boys lined a wall, with their hands in their pockets, trying to look cool. A teacher put on a record. Nobody danced.

Eventually the children were ordered onto the floor by a grinning, barking Mr Flyte, and the party got under way, with its usual succession of dances and savage games, winning, losing, tripping up, being humiliated. Tea-time came, and the Ghost had not appeared. Tim, Dorothy and Stephen exchanged hopeful glances over the sausage rolls. Perhaps he had gone ten-pin bowling after all. This was too much to hope for, of course, and as Miss Hooke struck up 'Jingle Bells' on the piano, and they all trooped back into the hall, he suddenly loomed up at Dorothy's elbow.

'Good afternoon, my dear,' he said. 'Having a jolly time?'

'It's all right,' muttered Dorothy, doing her best to get lost in the crowd.

While the children had been having tea, sweating teachers had been setting out chairs in rows, ready for the entertainment. There was now to be a half-hour sing-song, nobly led by Mr Flyte and Miss Hooke, while the rest of the teachers got their breath back over a cup of tea. Then the conjuror would appear, and at five o'clock Santa Claus would arrive to dish out toffees and balloons. After that, everyone would go home.

Dorothy managed to shake off the Ghost, getting herself wedged in the middle of a row between her friends Hannah and Wendy. The boys pretended they hadn't noticed him, but out of the tails of their eyes they all three watched him, leaning sinuously against the wall at the side of the hall, polishing his fingernails on the cuff of his purple velvet jacket. The other children could see him too, but they had got used to him. Except when he was doing something funny, like making Flytie sit down in a bowl of custard, he was just 'The man from the Circus', or, 'Mr Tweedie's friend'. Not one of them had ever noticed that his transparency had nothing to do with paint.

Mr Flyte, who fortunately could not see him, got up on the platform and adjusted his paper hat. He hated Christmas, and he had a headache coming on, but he told himself that it was all part of the job, and next week it would be the holidays. And in January he would set exams, and wipe the grins off all these happy faces.

'Right then,' he bawled, just as if he were calling his class to order on a Monday morning. 'Let's get started. All got your song-sheets, have you? Then we'll begin with "Rudolph, the Red-nosed Reindeer". Ready, Miss Hooke? Off we go!'

It was all the usual stuff, 'Rudolph', 'Good King Wenceslas,' 'I'm Dreaming of a White Christmas'. The children sang because it passed the time, and the Ghost sang along with the numbers he knew, the ones composed before 1900. But the chairs were hard, and the children got restless, so everyone was relieved when the other teachers came back from their tea. Mr Flyte descended from the platform, and Mr Tweedie, the headmaster, got up.

'Everyone having a good time?' he beamed.

'Ye-e-es,' they all droned dutifully, because they liked Mr Tweedie.

'Then here's a treat for you,' said Mr Tweedie, just as if everybody hadn't known since October what the treat was going to be. 'We have with us this afternoon a conjuror, a young lady who is making a fine reputation for herself in the circus, on stage, and on TV. Now, boys and girls, let me hear a nice loud round of applause for – *Miss Kitty Katz!*'

Dorothy could not clap, for her hands felt as if they were glued together. In a flutter of panic, she saw Kitty Katz, in her velvet tail-coat, tights and top hat, bound onto the platform, throwing up her hands and smiling a wide, lipsticky smile.

'Thank you, thank you, everybody!' she cried. 'Now, I want to introduce to you my assistant, who is also my young brother. A big hand, please, for Little Billy Katz!'

As Billy ran on-stage, twirling hoops and looking cute, Dorothy summoned courage to look at the Ghost. To her surprise and relief, he was not looking vengeful. Perhaps he had decided that Kitty was not to blame for Pussy's mistake of judgement all those years ago. He was staring at Kitty, certainly, but Dorothy was not close enough to see the expression in his eyes, which was very mischievous indeed.

Kitty did a few tricks, the usual kind with cards and silk handkerchiefs and a droopy rabbit. She did some juggling, and, having convinced her audience that a painted box was empty, produced from it an enormous tissue-paper flower. It was all pretty tame, and the children began to shuffle, and wish it was time for Santa Claus to come. Not until Kitty and Billy wheeled a long box like a red and green striped coffin onto the platform, and Kitty produced a large, sharp-toothed saw, did a ripple of pleasure run round the hall. The children sat up and took notice again. But when Kitty called brightly for a volunteer to be sawn in half, enthusiasm quickly ebbed. It is much more amusing to see someone else being sawn in half than to be sawn in half yourself.

'One of the teachers, then?' suggested Kitty hopefully. 'Oh, come on! Be sports! It's the kiddies' Christmas!'

The teachers, who did not need this reminder, responded negatively. The children looked fixedly at Mr Flyte, but Mr Flyte was taking no chances. He stared at the ceiling, then at the floor. But, at this awkward moment, the Ghost rolled himself off the wall, strolled up onto the platform, and bowed to Miss Kitty Katz.

'Madam, you may cut me in half,' he said.

The children roared approval, while the teachers, who could see nothing, glanced at one another in nervous perplexity. They were outnumbered by thirty to one, and they hoped the ranks were not going to become obstreperous. They watched the children suspiciously, but seeing no sign of a riot, wisely sat tight.

Kitty stared at the Ghost. She knew that she had seen this strange fellow before, and thought vaguely that he had something to do with a funny turn she had had one night at the Circus. But, for the moment, she could remember no more than that. Anyway, if he was the only one of this miserable shower willing to be sawn in half, she would saw him in half. The show must go on.

At a nod from his sister, Billy opened the box, and the Ghost, who was an old trouper, made a great show of terror before jumping lightly in. Sticking his head out of the hole at the top, he made faces and blew raspberries at the children, and waggled his feet through the hole at the bottom. Billy put on the lid, and Kitty inserted her saw into a groove which ran round the middle of the box. The Ghost, who was in his element, roared out a song from his Music Hall days, as she laboriously sawed right through the box.

> *'Roamin' in the gloamin',*
> *By the bonnie banks o'Clyde,*
> *Roamin' in the gloamin'*
> *Wi' a spookie by my side . . .'*

Kitty, aware that she was being upstaged by her stooge, looked glum, but there was nothing she could do about it.

The children were half amused and half horrified, and when Kitty and Billy separated the two halves of the box, and turned them around so that the Ghost's feet touched his head, one of the little children began to wail, and had to be taken on his teacher's knee, and comforted. What made it worse was that the Ghost, showing off like crazy, went on singing,

> *'. . . When the sun has gone to rest,*
> *That's the time that I love best,*
> *In a nookie wi' my spookie*
> *In the gloamin'!'*

But then, with a flourish, the box was put together again, the lid removed, and Kitty stood aside,

expecting that her victim would climb out, to relieved and delighted applause.

What she did not know, of course, was that the Ghost was an illusionist too, and a ghost besides. To her utter astonishment, and to the children's horrified delight, the Ghost got out of the box in two halves. While his trousers and feet did a tap-dance on the left of the platform, the top half of his body floated on the right. Taking a cigar out of his pocket, he lit it with a match, and blew hundreds of smoke-rings all round the hall. Then he came together again, and bowed, and bowed, and bowed. The children cheered, while Kitty and Billy clapped sportingly. The teachers, who had seen nothing but a girl sawing an empty box in two, looked at their watches and thought how lovely it would be to go home to bed.

10   Excursion Day

The Ghost went off-stage with Billy and Kitty
Katz, and the children did not see him again that
day. On Sunday morning, however, he put in an
appearance in the Bonellas' living-room, where
Dorothy was making Christmas cards with cra-
yons and sticky paper, while Tim and Stephen
did their homework. Christmas or not, Mr Flyte
was still piling on the homework, and Stephen
had come over to check his Maths answers against
Tim's. They were having trouble with a question
about the different amounts of fuel used by a
juggernaut and a Mini on a journey round the
equator. Tim said it was this kind of question
which proved Flytie was completely off his head.

The children had got so used to the Ghost's
arriving through the wall that they scarcely took
any notice. He seated himself in his favourite
chair, and took out a half-finished sleeve of Aggie
the wraith's pink jumper. After he had waited
some time, in vain, for congratulations on yesterday's exhibition to gush forth, he was obliged to
ask, archly, 'And did everyone enjoy the party, I

wonder? Did the *conjuring* give satisfaction?'

There were half-hearted grunts from the boys, who were trying to reconcile 57.183 litres (Stephen's answer) with 995,807.776 litres (Tim's answer). Dorothy said, 'Oh, yes, Mr Porrex. Lovely,' and licked a small ghost, which she then stuck down on top of a Christmas tree. 'This is for you,' she added.

'Charming,' responded the Ghost politely, but his mind was not on Christmas cards. He decided on the direct approach.

'I spent the night at Kitty's place,' he announced baldly. Pencils and scissors fell onto the table, eyebrows shot up, and the children gave him all the attention he desired. 'She invited me back after the show. Once she had taken on board that ghosts are good for you – I did save her paltry act, after all – she became very friendly. She's in theatrical digs in Helsinki Place, while the Circus is off the road for the winter, and it was just like old times. Three-legged beds and a kipper for your tea – not that I partook, of course. Afterwards, in the parlour, we had a long, interesting chat. She told me that she did indeed have a great-great-auntie Pussy in a Very Old Folks' Home in Liverpool. A hundred and eight last August, and still very spry. Kitty thinks she'd be delighted if I paid her a visit—' The Ghost guffawed, and the children looked disapproving.

'Does Kitty know about your – um, accident?' asked Tim.

'No, she does not know about my – um, accident,' retorted the Ghost testily. 'Nor does it seem to me proper to inform her. I did, however, question her very carefully on the subject of wands.'

'And?' prompted Stephen.

'And I drew a blank,' admitted the Ghost disappointedly. 'Kitty had never heard her Auntie Pussy, or any other member of the Katz family, mention a wand which had once belonged to the greatest magician the world has ever known. As for her own, it is of no antiquity. She bought it along with some other props from a Tricks shop in Clacton-on-Sea. So now I know that Pussy did not steal my wand, as I have sometimes suspected. God forgive me,' he concluded unctuously.

'So what now?' asked Dorothy, at a loss.

'Over to you again,' replied the Ghost, beginning to decrease at the armhole.

Before he went off to listen to the Salvation Army Band playing carols in the park, however, the Ghost told the children an astounding piece of news. They never knew how he got his information, but supposed it had to do with his ability to go through walls, and be invisible. However it was, he was very rarely wrong.

The news was that Big Pinky Mackintosh, now recovered from his illness, would not be rejoining the Phantoms. He had taken out his ear-studs, removed the ring from his nose, and was growing his hair. He had been seen dressed in a grey suit, carrying his mother's shopping basket, and was talking about going to University next year to study Medicine. The reason for this dramatic conversion, apparently, was a warning he had had from Dr Stookie when he saw him at the Health Centre, that his present lifestyle would bring him to a sticky end.

The Ghost said he only hoped Pinky understood that when he was a doctor he would not be qualified to make bad smells, or treat difficult patients with exploding sausages.

'But that's wonderful, Mr Porrex,' said Dorothy,

beaming. 'Now you only have five Phantoms to frighten.'

'When you find my wand,' said the Ghost pleasantly.

As always, when this subject was raised, a grey depression settled on the children. Now that it was dark when they went off to school in the morning, and getting dark when they came home in the afternoon, it was impossible to search further on the site of the Baltic Theatre. Besides, they had been over the ground not once, but several times now, and finding a needle in a haystack would have been a much simpler task. And they just had no idea where else to look.

Yet the problem of the Phantoms did not go away. Their number might be reduced to five, but that was still five too many.

On Monday, which was the second-last day of term, lessons at Harbour Green School were suspended for what was called Excursion Day. The smallest children were taken to a Puppet Show at the Jubilee Hall, but for the older ones – Dorothy's class and upwards – there was a choice of outings, this year either to the Roman Fort, or to the Town Museum. When it had been established that Mr Flyte was to be in charge of those going to the Roman Fort, Tim, Stephen and Dorothy opted for the Museum. In charge of this group would be Mr Cardew, of class 6C, a mild and gentle lamb compared with Flyte.

On the bus, Mr Cardew distributed activity sheets and pencils, and told the children about the various exhibitions, 'Prehistoric Life', 'Egyptians', 'Vikings', 'Transport through the Ages', 'Kings and Queens', 'Costume', and 'Great Scottish Inventions'. 'You must choose three,' said Mr Cardew. 'Look at the exhibits, and fill in your sheets. Meet at the Cafeteria for lunch at 12.15. All right? Oh, and one other thing. If you have any spare time, you might like to have a quick look at this month's special exhibition in Gallery Four. It's called "Scottish Theatre, 1540–1980".'

'Thank God we didn't tell old Porridge we were coming here today,' said Stephen fervently to Tim, as the bus drew up in front of the Museum. 'Imagine him at a Theatre Exhibition! He'd be giving guided tours.'

Inside the Museum the children scattered, while Mr Cardew and Miss Wilkins went off to the Cafeteria for their morning coffee. Dorothy tagged along after Stephen and Tim, lazily copying what they wrote on their sheets. They went from 'Prehistoric Life' to 'Vikings', then to 'Great Scottish Inventions', where there were models you could work by pushing buttons on the sides of the showcases. The activity sheets were easy, and they had finished by ten to twelve.

'Might as well have a look at the theatre stuff,' said Tim, so they followed the arrows, and found themselves in a long, darkened gallery with lighted showcases down either side.

It was all chronologically arranged. There was a model of what might have been the first Scottish theatre, and frail costumes worn at a performance of Shakespeare's *Hamlet* in Glasgow in 1781. There were photographs of pantomime dames, Harry Lauder's walking-stick, and a pair of faded pink ballet shoes belonging to Anna Pavlova, a great Russian dancer who had performed in Scotland in the 1930's. But none of this interested the children greatly, and they were just about to go and have another squint at the dinosaurs when suddenly Dorothy squeaked, 'Tim! Stephen! Come and look at this!'

Alerted by the excitement in her voice, the boys hurried over, and joined her in front of a glass partition. Behind it was an exhibit labelled, 'The Baltic Theatre: A Great Scottish Music Hall.'

'Christmas!' breathed Tim, appropriately. The three children stared in fascination into the illuminated box. Pinned onto a back-cloth of draped red velvet were black-and-white photographs of performers whose names Tim and Dorothy remembered the Ghost mentioning on the first night they met: Vesta Tilley, Dan Leno, Harry Lauder, Marie Lloyd. And yes! There was The Great Porrex, looking only slightly more solid in life than in death. There was also another conjuror called Chung Ling Soo.

'He's not Chinese,' said Stephen contemptuously, disliking the crudely made-up face.

There was a nice little pasteboard model of the theatre, with a flagpole on top. There were dolls, dressed in Harlequin costumes, old programmes, a playbill advertising *Mother Goose*. But the children's eyes were drawn in amazement to a green baize-covered board, down in the front right-hand corner of the case. To it were pinned some newspaper cuttings, yellow with age:

'TRAGEDY AT THE BALTIC' said one headline. 'MAGICIAN'S FATAL FALL' said another. Peering closer, the children read these words:

'Last night at the Baltic Theatre, Baltic Lane, a tragic accident occurred. Sidney Marmaduke O'Learie (45), better known by his stage name, "The Great Porrex", fell to his death in the course of an act which he had completed successfully on many occasions.'

There was much more, but the children did not bother to read on. They knew the story already. Besides, simultaneously they had noticed something else.

Beside the board, on a purple velvet cushion, lay a black lacquered stick, twenty-five centimetres long, topped with a gilded knob, and adorned with three bands, two silver and one gold. A small, printed card of explanation lay beside it:

Magician's Wand, late 19th Century
This wand was the property of the
late 'Great Porrex'
Found at the scene of his accidental death
27 December 1900
Lent by Mr John Whitehead

'I don't know who Mr John Whitehead is,' said Stephen, shaking his head ominously, 'but I wouldn't like to be in his shoes when old Porridge hears about this.'

But all that Dorothy could say, as she hopped from one foot to the other was, 'We've found the wand! We've found the wand! We've found the wand!'

11   Christmas Eve

'I only hope this is going to be all right,' said Stephen fervently. They were sitting upstairs in a green city bus, trundling up town to Albert Square, where the Museum was. 'I don't want to be arrested on Christmas Eve. My mum would go bananas, and I wouldn't get my new bike tomorrow.'

'It would be good-bye to my skateboard, too,' admitted Tim. 'But I don't see what else we could do. I mean, we couldn't *not* tell him we'd found it. If anything goes wrong, we'll just have to pretend we don't know him, and walk away.'

'If anything goes wrong,' said Dorothy mournfully from the seat behind, 'he won't even *have* to walk away. He'll go invisible, and we'll be left with the explaining to do.'

'Gee, thanks a bunch,' growled Tim.

The Ghost was sitting at the front of the bus with his feet up on the window ledge. He loved what he called 'horseless omnibuses', especially if he could go on the upper deck. Sometimes he pretended he was driving, making 'brr-oom,

brr-oom' noises, and turning an imaginary driving-wheel. But today he was preoccupied, fidgeting, and tutting impatiently whenever the bus stopped to take on more passengers. The children noticed that no one ever tried to take the seat where he was sitting. He was invisible, but perhaps people sensed a presence.

The Ghost had been away for a couple of days on a quick haunt to Aberdeen, to see Aggie. On his return the previous evening, the children had broken to him the good news that his long-lost wand had been found. They had expected him to zoom off immediately to the Museum to recover it, but his reaction had been more cautious.

Looking suspicious, he had made them describe the wand in minute detail, and tell him exactly what it had said on the little card.

'I don't altogether trust you,' said the Ghost. 'Your anxiety to get rid of your oppressors—' he never called them 'Phantoms' if he could avoid it '—might make you try to fob me off with some similar but inferior wand.'

'Would we do that?' said Tim indignantly.

'Yes,' said the Ghost.

'It said it was yours,' sighed Stephen. 'Why don't you take a flitter up to the Museum now, and see for yourself?'

'I have waited since 1900,' said the Ghost loftily, 'and I can wait another day. Tomorrow, we shall all go together – then you can have the pleasure of seeing me recover my property. And if you have tricked me—'

'We haven't tricked you,' they groaned.

'Good,' said the Ghost, with menace.

They could, they knew, have refused to go. But secretly, Stephen and Tim were dying to see how the Ghost would recover his property from inside a locked glass case, so they said they would go along, despite the risk. And Dorothy, who thought she knew how he would do it, wanted to go to see whether she was right. Her only fear was that he might activate the burglar alarm. There was something very electric about the Ghost.

They got off the bus outside the Museum, a great red sandstone building made in imitation of an Italian palace. With the Ghost ahead of them, looking jittery, they climbed a long flight of steps to the revolving door, pushing through into the huge galleried hall, with its display cases and stern warnings not to touch.

'This way,' said Tim, and led the Ghost up the main staircase, past the large-eyed, watchful mummy-cases in the Egyptian room, and up a further stairway to the darkened gallery where the Theatre Exhibition was. There were very few people about, but that was small comfort. Uni-formed attendants could loom up with the sudden-ness of ships in a fog, and no doubt the whole place was wired up, ready to go off like hell's bells if you so much as sneezed.

'Where is it?' whispered the Ghost harshly. 'Where is my wand? Is it at hand?'

Even Tim felt sorry for him. He was in a terrible state, shaking like a net curtain in a draught, and the children could see hope, fear, doubt and longing conflicting on his pale, spectral face.

'It's all right,' said Tim reassuringly. 'Keep cool. It's over here. Come and see.'

Hardly daring to look, the Ghost allowed him-self to be led to the showcase where the relics of the Baltic Theatre were displayed.

'Look,' said Dorothy, pointing.

There was a pause, then a delighted radiance

lit up the Ghost. A faint pinkness suffused his face, and his aura came on, lighting up the dark gallery with a golden glow.

'It is indeed my wand,' he said. 'I must seek out and thank the kind gentleman who has kept it safe for me. And I thank you too, from the bottom of my heart.'

For the Ghost, it was a most gracious speech.

Then the Ghost put out his hand lightly, and the children drew in their breath, waiting for the clamour of bells which would begin the ghastly process of arrest, interrogation and the confiscation of their Christmas presents. But they need not have worried. Someone who could walk through walls could also put his hand through glass. He did so, lifted the wand very delicately, and drew it back through the glass towards him.

'I have it,' he confirmed. 'Now – let me see.' Taking one end of the wand in each hand, he made a twisting movement, then tugged, and the wand came apart in the middle. As the children watched in fascination, the Ghost slipped the half with the gilt knob into his pocket, and up-ended the bottom half over the palm of his left hand. He shook, and something shiny fell out. With a cry of joy he spun it brilliantly in the air, catching it as it fell between finger and thumb.

The children gasped. It was a golden ring, set with a diamond so large you could scarcely believe it was real.

'It was the safest place I could think of,' explained the Ghost. 'A fine gem, is it not? It was bequeathed to me by my grandmother, lovely Millie Cornelia, the Piccadilly Nightingale. She had it from a Russian prince, she told me, whom she had enchanted with her songs. And now—' he beamed delightedly '—it will be my Aggie's engagement ring!'

With these words, he vanished.

Slowly, the children turned back to the lighted showcase, Tim and Stephen fully expecting to see the velvet cushion empty. Dorothy, who had realised on the night of the Circus that things which the Ghost touched were as ghostly as he was, was less surprised to see that the real wand lay there still, undisturbed. She was not going to boast to the boys about her superior brains, however. They would pull off her hair-ribbon, and call her Smartypants, and say she was just being wise after the event. She would wait until she was grown up, then beat them at everything.

They stared at the wand for a long time. Then Tim said, 'But surely – if there was a ring in the ghostly wand—'

'Should we tell the man at the desk?' wondered Stephen.

Dorothy said, 'But how could we possibly explain?'

'You mean, how we knew?'

'Yes.'

They decided that it was far too complicated. Mr John Whitehead would have to find out for himself. It was not their business, and tomorrow was Christmas Day.

'Let's go home,' said Tim.

The Ghost was waiting at the bus-stop.

'On Boxing Day,' he promised, 'I shall repay.'

'Thanks,' they said.

12   The Ghost's Grand Finale

It was the best Christmas Day ever. Tim got his skateboard, Stephen his new bicycle, and Dorothy the dolls' house she had always wanted. The Tartan Parrot was closed for the day, and at noon Mrs Cheng, Stephen and Alice arrived, with the Ghafoors from the Pakistani restaurant round the corner. They had a proper Christmas dinner in the living-room, with crackers, and turkey and plum-pudding on china plates. Whey they had all stuffed themselves to capacity, Mrs Cheng said that the next party would be at her place, to celebrate the Chinese New Year. So there was still something to look forward to.

After dinner, while the grown-ups washed up and drank coffee in the kitchen downstairs, the children played party games with the Ghost, who appeared through the wall wearing a spectral paper hat. They played 'Blind Man's Buff' and 'Hunt the Thimble', which the Ghost remembered from his childhood, and 'Musical Bumps', which he loved. The Ghost was so happy that he didn't even take offence when Tim told him a tasteless joke. 'Mr Porrex, where should you go when you're dying? Into the living-room!'

Before he left, the Ghost said, 'Thankyou', politely for the party, and added that he would see the children again next day.

'I reckon it'll be our turn for a visit from the Phantoms tomorrow,' Tim told him. 'They haven't been to our place for nearly two weeks.'

'I shall be behind the fringed curtain in the restaurant at half-past six,' promised the Ghost. 'I'm looking forward to it.' He was not the only one.

Tim was right. The Phantoms arrived at the Tartan Parrot on Boxing Day at ten to seven, roaring up on their motor-bikes in a dazzle of bewildering light. They parked on the pavement, took off their skull-and-crossboned helmets, and swaggered menacingly into the café. Jake Gorman, their leader since Big Pinky's resignation, goose-stepped up to the counter, while his four companions in crime lounged up against the wall, kicking the paintwork with their sharp-toed boots. Jake stretched over the counter, and helped himself to a handful of chocolate biscuits, which he stuffed into his pocket.

'Five fish suppers with extra chips, Mrs,' he snarled, in his best Pinky imitation. 'And hurry up. We can't hang around in this dump all night.'

Mrs Bonella didn't bother to argue. She was afraid of having her café vandalised if she did, but much more afraid that her children would be harmed. She couldn't afford to give away free food, but there was nothing she could do about it. She knew that even now, Mr McNabb would be telephoning the police, but by the time action was taken, the Phantoms would be far away. She did not blame the police, who had far too much to do.

Wearily, Mrs Bonella lifted a cardboard container, and opened the steel door of the heated cupboard where she put the fish to keep warm.

'Big ones, mind,' warned Jake menacingly, while the other Phantoms sneered and snarled in the background.

But before Mrs Bonella had time to lift the first fillet of fish with her tongs, the Ghost struck. Tim, Stephen and Dorothy, crouching in the dark at the foot of the house stairs, first saw a flash of green light, then heard a noise like growling thunder. The fringes of the curtain went from vertical to horizontal, as an icy wind blasted through the shop. Reams of wrapping paper and cardboard plates rose into the air, and were tossed around the shop like autumn leaves. The wind also lifted the Phantoms clean off their feet, and deposited them in a sprawling heap on the pavement outside.

'Help!' they yelled. 'What's happening? Help!'

No help came. The Phantoms scrambled to their feet and rushed to their motor-bikes, leaping astride and kicking furiously to spring them into life. But, of course, they would not start. The Ghost had seen to that. Then they saw him. Red-eyed and ghastly green-faced, pointing skeletal fingers, he bore down upon them, shrieking, 'Woo, woo, woo-oo-oo!'

'Oh, God,' moaned the Phantoms. 'What's this? Murder! Help! Police!'

It was the first time in their lives that the Phantoms have ever called on the police for help, and the response was the same as it had been for all the people who had called the police for protection against them. Leaping off their lifeless motor-bikes they bolted down the pavement, howling and bumping into annoyed passers-by.

'Hooligans! Young people nowadays!' said the passers-by. 'Did you hear thunder?'

'I thought I saw lightning.'

'Funny weather for the time of year!'

The Ghost pursued, unseen by anyone except the Phantoms themselves, and the children, who had run to the café door to watch.

'Good old Porridge!' they shrieked. 'Go on — let them have it! Hooray!' The Ghost needed no encouragement. He was giving the performance of his life.

Down one side of Baltic Street he chased the Phantoms, then, blocking the exit, chased them back up the other. Green and orange by turns, crackling electrically, wailing like an ambulance siren, he was everywhere they turned. Firecrackers

exploded under the Phantoms' feet and sulphurous snakes appeared out of the air, hissing and twisting around their heads.

'Help!' they bawled. 'Help! Mummy! Daddy! Police! Help!'

But neither mummies, daddies nor policemen came to their aid.

Mrs Bonella came to the door of the café, wielding a broom. She was sweeping up the cardboard and paper which lay in drifts on the floor.

'Just my luck,' she complained. 'A tornado hits Baltic Street, and whose shop does it have to come whirling through? Mine. Never a mention on the weather forecast, of course. And what on earth is the matter with these young men? You'd think all hell was after them.'

The children were too preoccupied to comment on this remark. They were watching the fireworks, and listening gleefully to a warning, wooing and wailing as the Ghost took his revenge.

> *'Unless your wicked ways you mend,*
> *Prepare to come to a sticky end!'*

The Ghost was not the greatest poet in the world, but the Phantoms got the message.

'Yes, yes,' they whimpered exhaustedly. 'We'll mend our ways. Only let us go home!'

At length, the Ghost did. Slackening his pace, he left an opening for the Phantoms to escape

down Baltic Lane. The terror of his presence died away.

'Queer, that, wasn't it? No thunder and lightning forecast,' remarked a customer, coming into the Tartan Parrot to buy his supper. 'What they call a freak storm, I suppose.'

'I am *not* a freak,' said the Ghost, offended. He had just popped back for a moment to collect his knitting.

Next morning, when they were out shopping, the children saw the Ghost for the last time. He was standing with his carpet-bag at the bus-stop outside the Portly Puss, on the corner of Baltic Street.

They ran towards him, but before they could reach him, a Number 13 drew up at the stop. The Ghost hopped in, winked, waved through the window, and was gone.